Forever Danish

excerpts from the novels

Amalie's Story

Petra

The Sailing Out

by

JULIE JENSEN McDONALD

Penfield Books

This book is dedicated to
my grandchildren and future generations
to whom Danishness is bequeathed.

Mette Marie Ibsen Faurschou,
Grandmother of Julie Jensen McDonald

Front cover: Myrtle Petra Faurschou and Alfred Julius Jensen on their wedding day, February 19, 1919, in Harlan, Iowa.

Back cover: Mary Julienne Jensen and Elliott Raymond McDonald, Jr. on their wedding day, May 6, 1952, in Iowa City, Iowa.

Editor: Joan Liffring-Zug Bourret
Copy editors: Melinda Bradnan, Dorothy Crum
and Lindsay Keast
Cover Design: Molly Cook, M.A. Cook Design
Interior Design: Kathleen Timmerman

ISBN 1-932043-36-5
Library of Congress Control Number: 2005905477

To Meet Queens

To meet Queens, go to forests.
Or, more exact, find yourself walking

in a high green Danish wood
of elms, of slim green-shaded elms

the delicate pallor of fish,
find yourself in this elegant

underwater-seeming Danish wood,
and there the Queens will come

to you, will touch
your tired forehead with white hands,

that head which is so tired,
with their white hands.

—Michael Dennis Browne

ABOUT THE AUTHOR

Julie Jensen McDonald was born in a farmhouse in Audubon County, Iowa, on the brink of the Great Depression. Her mother's parents came to Iowa from Denmark in the early 1880s, and her father came to the United States from there in 1906.

Her father died in a tractor accident when she was four, and she and her mother left the farm to live with her maternal grandmother in Harlan, Iowa. Her brother was born seven months after their father's death. She wanted to be a writer very early in life and remembers making squiggly lines that she called "a book" before she knew her ABCs.

She majored in journalism at the University of Iowa, and her first job after graduation was as Women's Editor at the *Register Republic* and *Morning Star* in Rockford, Illinois. She later wrote for the *Quad-City Times* in Davenport, Iowa, and then for the *Rock Island Argus* and *Moline Dispatch* in the Quad Cities, where she still writes columns, features, and reviews.

For 26 years she taught journalism at St. Ambrose University, and she has published more than 30 books, including novels, histories, and ethnic material. Four of her plays have been produced by community and junior theaters.

She attended the Iowa Writers' Workshop for a summer and has taught in the Iowa Summer Writing Festival and the Mississippi Valley Writers' Conference.

Serving as chair of the Iowa Arts Council for four years, she then participated in the council's Writers-in-the-Schools/Communities program.

She has been a trustee of the Davenport Art Museum and is on the board of the Midwest Writing Center and a member of the Literary Arts Committee of Quad City Arts.

An elder at St. Andrew Presbyterian Church, Davenport, she is a member of the Danish Sisterhood, P.E.O., the Iowa Press Women, and the Scottish American Society of the Quad Cities, and a clarinetist in the Bettendorf Park Band.

She and her husband, Elliott R. McDonald, Jr., live in Davenport with their Scottish Deerhound, Lochinvar. Their children are Beth Pearson and Elliott R. McDonald, III, and they have six grandchildren.

CONTENTS

Introduction

Although the trilogy is loosely based on the lives of my grandmother, my mother and me, I hadn't realized some of the similarities until I started to choose excerpts for this book.

Amalie's Story is set in nineteenth century Denmark, which would seem alien to me if my grandmother had not told me tales of her homeland when I was growing up. The superstition about the wedding candle going out before midnight haunts my memory. The emigration to Iowa, the new life there, and Amalie's acceptance of the loss predicted by the candle complete that story.

In *Petra,* Amalie's youngest child is born after her husband's untimely death. Petra is a tomboy and a daredevil, the bosom buddy of her brother Stig. She becomes a schoolteacher and falls in love with Lauritz, a Danish immigrant. They buy a farm, where their long-awaited child, Margaret, is born. Like her father, Petra's husband meets an untimely death, and they leave the farm to live with Amalie.

The Sailing Out is Margaret's story. Born the year of the Crash, she sees hungry relatives come to the farm for a decent meal. Her grandmother teaches her not to lie by pricking her tongue with a pin when she tells a whopper. After her father's death, they move to town, where she expects to see a train coming down the street. Poor health during her childhood makes her an avid reader; she's never the belle of the ball, and she can't hope to go to college, but she gets a scholarship that makes anything seem possible. She takes her grandmother's advice, "Sail out!"

These three women share a zest for life and many of the same values in their early years, when they fall in love, and when they move on with the hand fate has dealt them.

—Julie Jensen McDonald

Birth and Early Years

from *Amalie's Story*

[I]

I WAS BORN IN THE REIGN OF Frederick VII of Denmark. In fact, the King and I shared the same birthday, October 6, and I was named Amalie after his queen, Caroline Amalie.

Danish women have been allowed to choose their own husbands since Viking times, and my mother, Bodil Ormstrup, was no exception. She fell in love with a peddler. Knowing that he met girls by the score as he carried his goods from place to place, she insured her niche in his memory by stitching her name on a cherry-colored ribbon and slipping it into his pack. The Ormstrups were not pleased when Bodil pulled Niels Ibsen back to her with that ribbon, but they respected her choice.

Bodil knew that the ribbon had done its work long before Niels Ibsen returned to her village. On Twelfth Night she followed the prescribed ritual of walking backward to her bed and throwing her shoe over her left shoulder as she prayed to the Three Holy Kings: "Whose table must I set? Whose bed must I spread? Whose name must I bear? Whose bride must I be?"

For a long time she could not sleep for excitement, but as she slipped over the blurred line between waking and sleeping, she saw a man coming toward her down a long, winding path. Her heart jarred against her ribs as she strained to recognize a face she could not see clearly. The man swung a pack down from his shoulders and dropped it beside the road, running to meet her unencumbered. Niels Ibsen's face was red-brown from a summer of walking from village to village with his wares. His eyes were blue as the Sound and full of love for her. The two did not touch in the dream, but when Bodil woke, she knew they soon would. She had faith in the Twelfth

Night formula, for no girl ever dreamed of any but her own true husband on that night.

Looking at a picture taken in my mother's girlhood, I have been certain that my father would have come back to her with or without the cherry-red ribbon, but the women of our family leave as little as possible to chance. Bodil's wide-spaced eyes were big and round with a look of merry wonder. Her lips were full, and her only stern feature was the straight nose that she had from her father, Henrik Ormstrup. Her waist was tiny, flaring to generous hips, and an embroidered shawl's crossed ends hugged a promising breast and a tidy rib cage. Her hair could only be guessed at, for she wore a bonnet with white side puffs showing only two pale, glossy wings pulled tightly from a center part. She was considered a beauty in her village.

Niels Ibsen was nothing to look at. He carried one shoulder a little lower than the other, even when his pack was put aside. His legs were very long, but when he sat in a chair he was no taller than a young boy. In the summer, he was swarthy as a gypsy from the heath, and his pale blue eyes seemed to leap from the dark face as a chimneysweep's do.

Why, then, did she love him? Because he carried the whole world in his pack; amber washed to our shores from southern forests, laces from Belgium that carried an excitement absent from our own Tønder lace, ribbons and gold braid from Paris, glass beads from Venice. His wares were pretty but forgettable. The tales he attached to them were what lingered in a house when he was gone.

"A long-dead tree has wept this tear for you," he would say, carefully placing a lozenge of amber in a young girl's palm, "a great pine that lived in the time of Thor and Odin. How the sea has shaped and smoothed it for your skin! Now for the chain. Perhaps the artisans of Amsterdam can serve you—their fingers are delicate and . . . ah, perfect!"

Bodil married her man of the world, and I was born at a decent interval. I was taken from my parents when I was less than two, and here is the fairy tale that was used to explain the circumstances to me. Must we have fairy tales to make reality bearable? My Uncle Karsten must have thought so. He told me this one.

He and his sister Bodil were very close when they were growing up. While tending the sheep together, they would talk and dream of the future, leaning against newly cut peat stacked in the shape of African huts.

Bodil filled her lap with daisies and wild carnations to weave into a crown while she spoke of a husband and a house filled with laughing children.

Karsten was more interested in sailing and ships, but he agreed that it would be pleasant to have a wife and children in port.

Uncle Karsten (though I never called him that) would hold me on his lap and tell this story about himself and my mother as if they were two other people he had known. He had a good lap. His thighs were round and padded, and they closed completely to make a secure resting place for me. He spoke so close to my ear that his tobacco breath stirred the tendrils of hair that escaped my tight braids, and I breathed shallowly to avoid missing a single word.

One day Karsten saw a lovely girl. She was Maren Borris, who had lived in the village always. They had known and greeted each other since childhood, but on this day she raised her eyes to his and they saw each other in a new way. They were the first to see the storks returning from Egypt on that April day, and everyone knows that the man who sees the father stork and the woman who sees the mother stork as they come back to their cartwheel nest—these two are fated to love each other.

Overwhelmed by his new obsession with Maren, Karsten no longer heard the crashing of the sea and the groaning call of ship's timbers. His horizons pulled in to the small triangle which Maren's feet traced between her father's farm, the village, and the step-gabled church.

He carved a *manglebroedt,* the traditional courting gift, which was a wooden rolling pin for squeezing the water out of clothes. Its handle was a horse in full gallop with the wind in its mane, and Maren's name was carved in bold, beautiful letters along its two-foot length.

On the day when the pastor donned his fat neck ruff and long gown to perform their marriage ceremony, Karsten said, "I could never wish for more than I have today!"

"Don't tempt fate!" Maren gasped, stopping his lips with her fingers, which he kissed.

While the vows were being spoken, one guest stood outside the church, clearly outlined in the sunny square of the open door. Karsten's head turned as by command, and when he saw the still form of Hansine, a half-witted girl who lived out on the heath, he scowled and tightened his fingers over Maren's. What was over was over.

Karsten and Maren moved into a pretty half-timbered cottage on her father's land. Maren's calm beauty grew riper as she cared for house and husband, and Valdemar Borris found a ready pupil in a son-in-law eager to learn the management of the farms.

At this point in the story, Karsten's voice would shift to a hushed minor. "But there was one thing they did not have—something dearer than comfort or gold—a child of their own." I would sit straighter on his lap, knowing that my own part in the tale was coming.

Bodil had not yet met her peddler, and she often visited her brother and his wife for a week or two at a time. One summer night Karsten asked her to come for a walk with him. Bodil turned toward Maren, thinking to ask her to join them, but Karsten shook his head, and they went out, leaving the wife in her kitchen.

Bodil did not take her brother's arm as she usually did when they walked, and he asked, "Are you cross with me?"

"It was unkind of you to leave Maren behind."

"It would be more unkind to make her listen to what boils up in me and must be said!"

"What on earth could that be?"

Walking ahead of her through the light, warm summer night, Karsten searched for words. A cuckoo called and the hollyhocks were dusky jewels against the walls of the cottage. The scent of the elder was strong in the air.

Bodil seemed to dismiss his urgency, rising on her toes to stretch her arms to the soft mauve sky and exult, "I love summer!"

"Summer or winter, what does it matter when you can't have what you want most?" Karsten cried. "We have no children, Bodil!"

She gave him a tiny push, mocking his self-pity. "If that's all you lack, Karsten, I'll have a dozen and give you one or two!"

"Promise me that!" He clutched her arm so tightly that he felt the shape of the bones beneath the rounded flesh.

Pulling herself free, she laughed. "I promise! Now, let's go back to Maren. She knows the Hedebo stitch, and I want her help with the cap I'm embroidering."

With Bodil's promise secured, Karsten and Maren worked hard to improve their circumstances. Karsten borrowed money from

Valdemar Borris to open a store in the village of Ausig twenty miles away. After a modest beginning, it flourished beyond their hopes.

When Karsten and Maren heard that Bodil was marrying a peddler, they feared for the quality of the promised child, but their impatience outweighed their doubts, and they traveled home for the wedding with great exuberance and hope.

Noticing Karsten's close inspection of her bridegroom, Bodil teased, "Would you like to see his teeth? You act like a buyer at a horse fair!"

"Surely you know why I look at him so closely?"

"If you look forever, you will never see what I see!" she said, laughing.

Karsten placed a muslin bag fat with seeds in her hands. "Maren and I follow the custom of Amager with this token of a bright, happy future—and the hope for many children."

"Seed?" laughed Bodil. "The Dutch of Amager are strange folk! I would prefer a bolt of fine linen."

"We have brought that too," Maren said with a slow smile, "but you must honor us by accepting this small gift as well."

Karsten and Maren walked to the long tables heaped with joints of ham, smoked legs of mutton, and prune tarts big as storks' nests. The first notes of the violins were sounding, and they watched approvingly as Niels Ibsen plucked the bag of seed from Bodil's hands and tossed it into a corner, then whirled her into a dance so breathless that her bridal wreath of myrtle nearly fell over her eyes.

"He is lively and she loves him," Karsten said.

Maren nodded happily. "It won't be long."

But it was three years before Karsten came to the home village again. Maren persuaded him to wait until the baby had a strong start in life before taking her from her mother. When the child was just beginning to walk and Bodil was pregnant with the next, Karsten made the all-important journey.

He arrived at night, for it took most of a day to drive from Ausig, and he took a room at the inn in the village. Though he knew that his sleeping under a strange roof would offend his sister, he couldn't risk being with her long enough to let her dissuade him from his intention.

In the morning he put on his shining Hessian boots and the green velvet coat with big silver buttons. He picked up his hat, then tossed it aside, not wanting Bodil to think he was putting on airs.

Harnessing his horse, he drove to Niels Ibsen's house and was shocked at the poorness of the home the peddler had provided for his sister. Without knocking, he flung the door open and looked straight into the face of Bodil.

She sat very still, hands folded over the vigorous movement of the unborn child.

"Well, Bodil, you look splendid!"

"Why did you spend the night under a strange roof? And where is Maren?"

Karsten saw that they were not alone. An ancient village gossip, whom everyone called Lillemor, was listening with keen interest, dipping almond *kager* in her coffee. Niels Ibsen stood at the hearth, filling his porcelain pipe.

"Lillemor, can you not come back another time?" Karsten said. "We have family business to attend to."

Reluctantly the old woman tied the ribbons of her cap and scuttled off to pass along the little that she knew. Karsten's fine and prosperous dress was enough to give her tongue a workout until she could wring something more from Bodil.

"Will your husband stay, Bodil?" Karsten asked.

"Why should he not?"

"Have you told him of your promise to me?"

Bodil looked bewildered. Then, as she started to understand, she swept up the toddler who was pulling at her skirts and held her so tightly that she cried in protest.

"A fine, healthy child, Bodil." Karsten touched the little girl's cheek, and she howled all the louder. "We will be able to do much for her. My business has prospered and I have bought a ship that sails from Aalborg to the Indies to bring back spices and silks." He looked around the long, low room with its tiny windows and timbered ceiling. The toe of his Hessian boot kicked at the dark earthen floor. "I have built a beautiful house for Maren—and Amalie."

"You wouldn't be so hard," Bodil whispered.

"You promised her."

"If I should have a dozen, I said—there is only Amalie!"

"Not for long. We knew you were with child, or I would not have come. I know it grieves you, but it is best for the girl. She is of my blood, Bodil!"

"And what of mine?" Niels Ibsen cried.

"Be sensible, man. Can you give her what I can?"

"Your stock may be larger than mine, but what do you know of a father's love?"

"More than you do, perhaps. To you, the feeling is as commonplace as the rain and the sun, but fatherly love has been my study. I have practiced it in my heart for years while I waited for this child."

"Bodil," Niels Ibsen said, "though this man is your brother, I shall take the poker to him!"

"Don't, Ib," she begged, "not if you love me! I gave Karsten such a promise, and what he says is true. Amalie will have a better life than we can give her. Please help me to my bed now, for I feel sick." She rose heavily, leaning on the arms of both men as she made her way to the curtained box bed in the next room. She turned her face to the wall and said, "Take her quickly! But be sure to tell her that she is mine and that I let her go because I wanted the best for her. Promise me that, Karsten!"

He did, of course, for ours is a promise-making family. This leads to sorrow more often than not, and I often consider swearing off promises, but I always go back to them. Promises keep a person striving.

According to Karsten, my parents were resigned to my going away, even glad about it when they had time to recover from the unexpectedness. I believed this for many years, and Karsten was the fairy-tale prince who rescued me from a dark hovel. He told me that I loved him very soon, before his liver-colored horse had carried us halfway to Ausig, and that I slept in perfect confidence, with my head resting on the green velvet joining of his hip and thigh.

We called this "Amalie's Story," and I preferred it to any of H.C. Andersen's tales, which pleased me well enough. Many years passed before I came to hear scraps of another version of it.

[2]

Coming to my new home so young, I had no dramatic first impression of Dovedale. Except for an occasional troubled dream, it seemed a place where I had always been. I was taught to call Uncle Karsten "Far" or Father and Aunt Maren "Mor," and I was at home.

The house at Dovedale was big and costly. Far had wanted a roof of rich, plum-colored tile, but Mor insisted that she must live under thatch as she always had, and he let her have her way.

Most of the substantial houses in Ausig had a sky-blue best parlor, but guests at Dovedale followed Hop-Caroline, the lame serving girl, to a drawing room with dark-patterned wallpaper, a richly decorated ceiling, and frescoes over the door.

I never visited this shadowed room alone. I was afraid without Koll, Mor's white Eskimo dog. He went in to sniff the furniture when the company had gone and protected me from the open-mouthed lions carved on the arms of the big, black sofa.

I was the only child anywhere near Dovedale, unless you counted Hop-Caroline. The sickness that had made her lame also left her somewhat simple-minded, and we were children together. When Mor drove away in her carriage to visit friends, Hop-Caroline would drop her goose-wing duster to play clapping games with me.

Mor kept Hop-Caroline as a charity, for the girl actually contributed very little to the running of the household. (We always called Hop-Caroline a girl, but she must have been older than Mor.) Mor attended to everything herself, moving briskly from room to room with a large ring of keys jingling at her belt. She made decorative molds of sweet butter; fat, round loaves of bread; towering whipped cream cakes; and vats of brown ale. She carded and spun wool, slaughtered and butchered pigs, and boiled linen sheets in a great tub. Her hands were never still, for when the big jobs seemed well under control, she snatched up her knitting needles or embroidery.

"You must watch and learn, Amalie," she would say, and I had my own small knitting needles before I could write my name.

I tried hard to please her, often despairing of satisfying her perfect standards. Mor was not patient.

My deepest disgrace came with the slaughtering of the fall pigs. Mor put on wooden shoes and tucked her skirt in the band of her long apron.

Pushing her sleeves above her elbows, she took a long, sharp knife from the kitchen table and said, "Come, Amalie."

Hop-Caroline put her weight on her short leg, tapping the foot of the longer one with excited anticipation. She loved slaughtering, butchering, and rendering, and she pulled me along as if we were going to a picnic. Though she was a pious Lutheran, Hop-Caroline wore a Thor hammer around her neck and embraced every superstition that came to her ears. On slaughtering day, she was Odin's daughter.

As we passed through the kitchen garden, the sleepy, spicy scent of the herbs had a mildly narcotic effect on my apprehension, but my fears sharpened again as we rounded the barn and saw Arne, the hired man, looping a rope around the back feet of a struggling pig. It was a pink, naked, human-looking pig, and its squeals were piteous.

Hanging the pig upside down from a strong beam, Arne stepped out of the way with a deferential nod to Mor. I saw the flash of her strong white forearm, the sun on the blade, and a gout of fantastically red blood. Hop-Caroline clapped her hands.

Bent double, I vomited until the lining of my stomach seemed to rise in my throat. I saw Mor's look of contempt through watering eyes and heard her say, "Take her away, Hop-Caroline, she is too young."

Weak and chastened, I spent the afternoon with Far, who devoted one day a week to repairing watches and clocks. He delighted in the intricacies of timepieces and sent Arne to all the fairs in the surrounding countryside to collect faulty clocks and watches. In a room set aside for the purpose he would diagnose and repair, charging the owners nothing for what he called his "pleasure."

The uncurtained room held the full light of the sun. Two long trestle tables were spread with dozens of carved clocks, pocket watches like gold onions, and dainty ladies' watches in cases of porcelain or silver. Far's big fingers moved among the tiny parts with incredible delicacy. The squint that held the jeweler's glass to his eye drew one corner of his mouth upward in a crooked smile.

I was not permitted to talk in this room, but I didn't mind. Far's happy absorption, the warm sun, and the many voices of time conspired to set me dreaming. I would harness Koll to a very small buggy and go to see what lay beyond the farthest hill visible from Dovedale. Away from the village and all the familiar things that forced him to be a common dog, Koll would speak like the animals in H.C. Andersen's tales. The black eyes that gleamed in his white-ruffed, wolfish head were so knowing that I was sure he would have much to say. Koll might be able to tell me who called to me in my sleep in a voice I knew but did not know. During these happy imaginings, it was easy to forget that Koll bit me when I disturbed his sleep and growled when I came too close to his food pan.

The men who came to visit Far were not invited to the clock room, and they had no liking for the formal sitting room. They would rest their elbows on the big dining-room table of Jacobean oak and talk or play poker, furtively claiming their winnings when Mor was not looking. Mor thought gambling was a sin, but a game of cards without stakes did not disturb her, and she would pass through the dining room from time to time to inspect the ale glasses, calling Hop-Caroline to replenish the ones that were empty.

I was allowed to play quietly in a corner of the dining room near the long windows when the men came until Mor heard me chanting a word I had picked up from the chairman of the Parish Council.

"Fordømmelse! Fordømmelse!" I repeated, laughing at the jarring, comic sound without the faintest notion that I was shouting "Damnation!"

"Who taught you that?" Mor demanded fiercely.

When I told her, her lips clamped tightly as a well-worked buttonhole. She left the room quickly, calling, "Karsten, I must speak to you!"

While they discussed my unsuitable utterance, I continued to enjoy a singsong repetition of it, and I was completely bewildered when Mor told me that I was not to go into the dining room when Far's friends came.

Missing the blue-gray layers of cigar smoke, the rich depth of male laughter, and the mingled smell of cognac and of boots that had passed through the barnyard, I found a hiding place behind the heavy drapes and enjoyed the forbidden company secretly.

As the weeks passed, the atmosphere changed, and with childlike self-importance, I thought my banishment was the cause. The men were more serious when they came, and they seldom played cards. They spoke of the death of King Frederick, the last monarch of the Royal House of Oldenburg. They worried about the discretion of the young King Christian IX. Making myself small behind the curtain, I listened to talk of General de Meza and *Dannevirke*; then of Dybboel and the Austrians and the Prussians, who were "the Devil's own."

When his friends left, Far would wander to his room full of timepieces, but he seemed to have little interest in them. He sat at the trestle table with his head in his hands and stared at the wintry fields outside.

"Are you sick, Far?"

"Mortally sick! Prussia-Austria has swallowed Slesvig, and the necks of Danes are under cruel boots. How long can Denmark survive?"

I didn't know what he was talking about, but I could visualize Arne, Hop-Caroline, Pastor Madsen, even Far and Mor, sprawled on the ground, with heavy boots pressing their faces into the dirt. My own neck hurt to think of it! As for somebody or other swallowing Slesvig, how could this be? Slesvig was a place far away, and it must be too big to swallow.

"Will the Austrians and the Prussians go to Hell?" I asked.

"They have come from Hell!" Far shouted, bulging the veins in his neck and spraying my face with saliva.

I had never seen him so upset, and I tried to think of a way to comfort him. I had been told of the statue of Holger Danske who slept with his beard growing into a table in a dungeon at Kronborg Castle. When Denmark was in terrible trouble, Holger Danske would rouse himself from his stony sleep and come to her aid.

"Why doesn't somebody go and tell Holger Danske?" I suggested timidly.

Far laughed as if his throat hurt. "Yes, why not? And we can call on Thor and Odin while we're at it!"

"Don't you think Holger Danske would come? Hop-Caroline told me he would if the trouble was bad enough."

"Don't believe everything that simple girl tells you," Far said, patting my head absently. "I must go to Aalborg. *Dronning Dagmar* will be due in port soon. I would like to sail away with her again! I cannot bear to see proud Denmark in this state!"

I looked through the windows, puzzled. "Everything looks the same to me."

"Because you are a child, you are spared much. Forget what I have said and play with Koll or Hop-Caroline. Even the nonsense of a simpleton is better for you than my bitterness! *Farvel,* Amalie."

I couldn't forget what he had said. The thought of boots on the neck and the swallowing of Slesvig gripped me while I helped Mor scrape carrots, while I knitted at a clumsy scarf, and when I lay in my featherbed at night looking at the stars through the small casement window of my room close under the thatch.

Far left for Aalborg in the box carriage with runners, driving an Iceland pony that took to the snow better than the liver-colored thoroughbred, Brand.

We all turned back to the house before he started up the far hill, for it was considered bad luck to watch a loved one out of sight.

"Which way is Kronborg *Slot,* Hop-Caroline?" I asked, as if I didn't care whether she answered or not, knowing this was the best way to get an answer, for she loved to tease.

She pointed vaguely to the southeast and hurried toward the house, blowing her breath in great clouds to show how cold she was.

I waited, kicking at the snow with my high boots, until she and Mor were safely inside. Then I took the wide road to the village. Wishing for Koll's company, I sadly renounced it. If I went to look for him, somebody would question me or hold me back.

Ausig was nearly two miles from Dovedale, and I was so tired when I got there that I hoped Kronborg Castle wasn't much farther. I walked down the one long, straggling street, and when I came to Far's store, I stepped inside, just to get warm. Dorotea Thomsen was busy selling calico, and I slipped behind the stove so she wouldn't see me and ask questions. I didn't want to leave the warmth and the mixed odors of soap, raisins, coffee, and tobacco, but I was in a hurry to reach Holger Danske. The bell above the door tinkled as I went out, and Dorotea called to me, but I didn't answer.

Beyond Ausig the road grew narrower. The sky darkened and it began to snow. The flakes came thicker and faster, clinging to my eyelashes and turning my red coat pink. With the sun hidden, I lost my direction and stumbled into a tiny lane where two men were digging with shovels. One wore big sea boots and the other had on wooden shoes and long, white woolen stockings pulled over his trousers to the knees. Both wore fur caps with flaps tied over their ears, and they looked like wild animals walking upright.

"Which way is Kronborg *Slot*, please?" I asked.

They leaned on their shovels and stared.

"Won't you tell me?" I was tired, half-frozen, and cross.

"Lille pige," said the man in wooden shoes, "little girl, this is no night for visiting castles! Does your mother know where you are?"

"Yes," I lied, "she sent me."

"Then she's a madwoman!" The man in sea boots spat into the snow. "You'd better come with us until the weather lifts." He dropped his shovel to hold out his arms, and I ran the other way.

I went on running with the muffled shouts of the men in my ears. Everything got whiter and whiter. The snowflakes seemed to whirl inside my head, and then there was nothing.

I woke in my own featherbed, hot and feverish. Something was holding me down, and I struggled until I realized that Mor was holding one of my hands and Pastor Madsen the other.

If the pastor was here in the night, it meant that death was in the neighborhood. I twisted my head to look at the window to see if the ice maiden was there reaching for me. Hop-Caroline had told me that the ice maiden took shape in the frost on the pane and stretched out her arms to receive the dying. The window was clear, so I sighed and drifted toward sleep as Pastor Madsen prayed over me and climbed back into the pastor's chair suspended in the wagon that drove him home.

Later I learned that Hop-Caroline had opened the casement and scraped the pane with a table knife, and I wondered how much of my recovery was due to praying and how much to paring.

I was well enough to sit up in my blankets by the time Far returned from Aalborg, and I spread the presents he brought me on the feather puff. There was a necklace of fish eyes iridescent with their retention of underwater mysteries, a length of cloth printed with strange shapes from the faraway islands, and a bag of rock candy.

I gave Far a kiss of thanks, and while my arms were around his neck, he asked, "Why did you run away, Amalie?"

To think that he would misunderstand me so! I swept the presents off the bed and refused to say a word. I never told him that I was going to Holger Danske. I have never told anyone until now.

In spite of my failure to reach the stone warrior, the spirits of everyone around me gradually improved. The men came to play cards again, and they spoke of reclaiming the heath, saying, "What is outwardly lost is inwardly won!"

When I asked Far what they meant, he said the bogs were being dried out and the heather cleared from the moors to make more land for growing things. They were trying to replace Slesvig, which the Austrians and Prussians had swallowed. He took me with him in the cart behind the Iceland pony to watch the laborious breaking of the heath and the planting of small pines in the ground torn from the heath's stranglehold.

I watched an old couple lifting their hoes high and bringing them down on the tough, matted growth with a stoic strength. Their faces were expressionless, as if they were resigned to an unrelieved lifetime of turf breaking.

Then Far told me of the mythical Gefion, who was offered as much of Sweden as she could plow in one night. She turned her sons into oxen and lashed them into plowing a great body of land that came to be called Zealand. The proof of this feat is a Swedish lake shaped just like Zealand.

"We could use some goddesses like that these days," he said, "men move too slowly."

"But we have longer than one night," I said.

"That is not for us to say."

[3]

When I was nine years old, my real father died. Far told me that we would not attend the funeral because my presence would only deepen Bodil's grief, reviving an old loss to keep the new one company.

I went alone to the village church and sat there trying to feel something. It was November, and the cold inside the church was like death itself. Even in the summer the bare, whitewashed walls were green with damp, and in winter the water in the font froze, and the pastor wore mittens in the pulpit.

In the gloomy light I could barely make out the White Christ on His cross, but I was sure that He could see me, and I was embarrassed that I could not squeeze out even one tear for my real father in His presence. The White Christ of Scandinavia is so different from the broken Saviour one sees in American crucifixes. The White Christ exults in His sacrifice with His head thrown back and His powerful hands thrusting upward with the nails, bearing them like a gift. He requires straightforward worship and fair dealing. I approached the altar cross to stand directly beneath His arching feet and confess my inability to manufacture grief.

Believing that He understood, I went out of the church relieved. Pastor Madsen was on his way in, and as we met, he asked if there were workmen inside.

"No, Pastor, I didn't see anyone—"

He frowned. "No time for God's work! The church can crack in two for all they care! You are a good girl to come when there is no service, Amalie; such piety is unusual in the young."

I explained about my real father dying from pneumonia, which he caught while walking from village to village in the fall rain. The pastor himself was coughing, but he leaned down to clasp my shoulder in sympathy.

"You will see him again, Child."

"But I haven't seen him the first time—not that I remember." I wanted to say more, but the pastor had returned to a worried scrutiny of the crack in the wall.

Pastor Madsen had no wife, but otherwise he seemed like other men when he wasn't wearing his ruff and clerical gown. He told jokes, drank ale, and played cards, laughing around the stem of a porcelain pipe. However, when he climbed the stairs to the high pulpit to preach and intone the liturgy, he seemed taller, thinner, and paler, and he had a way of pulling time out in a long, slender thread which I longed to break. Sometimes I felt as if I had gone into the church one day and come out the next.

The Sabbath began officially at noon on Saturday and ended on Sunday after the big meal in the middle of the day. The step-gabled church was as quiet as the neighboring graveyard until Sunday morning, when the carriages rolled up and the horses were tied to the low, iron fence.

The pumping of air over the condensed moisture in the organ pipes gave the slow hymns a watery quality that suited the undersea green of the light inside the church; sound and light all damply mingled. Stale air and prolonged droning put me into a dizzy trance that lifted only when we sat down to roast pork, red cabbage, rye bread, and Jutland rum pudding, with the guests Mor casually invited after the church services. The food was our means of returning to weekday heartiness, and as we ate, we recovered from the Sabbath as from an illness.

Mor was quick to take up her needle after the meal, having been without it for twenty-four hours. At Dovedale all sewing was put away at noon Saturday, as every Sabbath stitch had to be taken up with the nose in heaven. The moment Far pushed his chair back from the table, she snatched up her embroidery from the sideboard.

Far called for brandy and lit his pipe, addressing the pastor as he puffed. "I hear you have been to Vartov to hear Bishop Grundtvig preach since we saw you last. How did you find him?"

"He looked as old as Holy Canute come to life," Pastor Madsen said, "but there is power in him from beyond himself. In spite of all the unrest he has brought to formal Lutheranism, I cannot help but admire him. He is an inspired madman!"

I had seen pictures of N.F.S. Grundtvig and thought he was an ugly, old troll, but Far said he was right about educating the ordinary people and teaching them the wonderful stories of Denmark's past. It made them better humans.

Far's eyes narrowed and brightened with cheerful malice as he said, "I have been told of Grundtvig's inspiration—" he looked at me—"Amalie, please leave us."

I was accustomed to being ordered out when something unfit for young ears cropped up in the conversation, but I was nearly thirteen now and felt justified in leaving the room noisily, only to sneak back and listen at the door.

Mor scowled disapprovingly as Far told of the young Grundtvig falling in love with the mistress of a country house where he was employed as a tutor.

Far laughed richly. "The lady knew nothing of his passion, but Grundtvig was convinced that he was committing New Testament adultery, and he threw himself into the uplifting of Denmark to escape his besetting sin. There you have Grundtvig's inspiration!"

"The Lord works in unsearchable ways," Pastor Madsen said doubtfully.

Far had had his sport with Grundtvigdianere and jumped to the Home Mission people, saying, "The Indre Missioners won't admit to having bodies. It makes me want to smack their faces and prove that their non-existent flesh can feel pain! There's something wrong with people who call themselves 'We Holy Ones!'"

Mor seemed about to explode, but she only jabbed her needle savagely into the heart of an embroidered flower. Her mood was a disturbing surprise to Far, and he quickly changed the subject, calling me back to the table.

My confirmation was set for the second Sunday in October, a week after my thirteenth birthday, and I thought of it not as a witness to belief, but as a declaration of growing up. Confirmation would mean that I no longer would be sent from the room, whatever the subject. My hair would be put up and my skirts would be put down.

I had said my prayers since infancy and had grown into whatever faith I possessed gradually and painlessly. My confirmation would be just that—repeating to our friends and neighbors what they already knew about me, or thought they knew. Any dark doubts about my relationship with the Deity would remain my secret. It did not occur to me that others might have similar secrets.

The Saturday before my confirmation it rained until Hop-Caroline muttered about "God's Judgment." The storm was a long time coming and fiercer than any I remembered. The edge of the southwestern sky turned blood-red, then pale yellow, darker yellow, and finally blue-black with featherbed clouds that billowed and ruptured over Dovedale.

I threw open my window to lean into the wall of water, and something pagan possessed me. When the lightning speared the fields, when Thor hammered out his thunder, I wanted to shout. Mor frowned at my wild face as she pulled me inside and scolded me for getting my hair wet.

Peeking from under the towel as I dried myself, I saw her looking at me with the expression she wore when she glimpsed the gypsies on the heath—a look that was two parts disapproval and one part fear with a hint of curiosity thrown in for good measure.

She hung my confirmation dress on a wall peg and touched the gold-embroidered border at its hem. Puffing the long sleeves of the bodice and flattening the round lace collar with careful fingers, she said, "I will hear your prayers for the last time tonight, Amalie, tomorrow you will be responsible for your own soul."

I knelt for the childish prayer that was so familiar that it meant no more than the warmth of the feather bed or the steady glow of the beeswax candle beside my bed. The pastor had told me that I must put away childish things. Knowing it was the last time, I nearly wept through the brief, rhyming petition, "Jesus keep me all the night, set my feet in paths of right . . . "

At the end, I took Mor's hand to ask her forgiveness for everything I had done wrong that day. She had taught me not to let the sun go down without making peace with everyone, and since everyone was not at my bedside, Mor was the stand-in for my entire small world.

On this night I asked forgiveness for my obscure rebellion in the storm, for shouting at Hop-Caroline when she accidentally stuck me with a pin during the last fitting of my confirmation dress, and for telling Hanne Eskildsen that my confirmation presents would be nicer than hers. I watched Mor's face closely to catch the shadowy smile that told me my sins were insignificant, even adorable.

She wouldn't look at me, and as she pried my fingers loose, she said, "We have raised you no better than Koll, and if your soul is blemished, it is our doing!"

"What do you mean?" I cried. "There's nothing wrong with my soul! I'm going to be confirmed tomorrow!"

"I have looked into your eyes, Amalie, and what I see there frightens me."

"What do you see? What?"

"The Devil—he looks out of your eyes, and you must fight him hard!"

"That's not the way Lutherans talk, Mor!"

She smiled then, but it was a terrible smile. "I am glad that you see my difference! After tomorrow, I will tell everyone and stop the lying hypocrisy of my life! Outwardly I have been an orthodox Lutheran, but my heart is with the Indre Mission!" She blew out the candle and stood for a moment in the doorway, her strong face silhouetted by the candles in the hall. I was afraid of her, and when a flash of lightning bathed her features in apocalyptic light, I pulled the covers over my face to escape her burning eyes.

In the morning I thought I had dreamed it all. Mor came into my room with chocolate and bread with jam as soon as I awoke, and when Far brought my gifts, she smiled while I opened them. Mor's gift was an amber cross to wear around my neck, and Far's was an elegant folding fan from Spain. Hop-Caroline had tatted lace to edge a fine, white handkerchief for me.

After Mor and Hop-Caroline helped me dress and put up my hair, I walked very carefully down the stairs, thinking that the new weight of my piled hair was quite uncomfortable. A gold-edged bonnet with ribbons held it all in place, however, and by the time I climbed into the carriage to drive to the church, I was turning my head as easily as ever.

The sun had come out to dry up most of the heavy rain, leaving sparkling pools between the cobbles. The tree trunks were washed to a wet dark brown the color of soaked cinnamon, and the sky was October blue at its heart-tearing best.

Far was happy and proud, shouting his greetings to everyone we passed, "Good day and God help!" He smiled at Mor, who sat beside him in the carriage straight-shouldered and reserved.

Why couldn't she share his bursting joy? What locked her away from the pleasures of living? I remembered then that she had given me an answer the night before, but the chilling thought of the Indre Mission made me try to think of something else.

The service in the church seemed longer than usual, probably because I knew everyone was watching me and couldn't allow myself to drift into dreams. I was tempted to imagine myself small enough to run along the gold serpentines of my skirt border, but I resisted this alluring fancy.

Afterwards, everyone congratulated me, and I walked among the gravestones and markers while Far and Mor talked longer with their friends. I stooped to read the lettering on my favorite scrolled cross. *"Tak for Alt,"* it said. "Thanks for Everything." This was a common inscription that strongly appealed to me. I considered it a pleasant leave-taking.

Feeling a tug at my bonnet strings, I turned to see Birch Sandahl's round face grinning at me. Birch was in my class at the village school, and he always tripped and pushed me.

"Stop that, Birch Sandahl!" I pulled the ribbons from his fingers angrily.

He caught my wrists and planted a wet kiss on my mouth. "How do you like my confirmation gift, Amalie?"

I scrubbed at my lips with Hop-Caroline's gift, and, seeing nothing in his hands, gathered his meaning. Boys were worse than pigs! If that was a kiss, I might go with Mor to the Indre Mission and give up kissing forever!

"You're pretty with your hair up, Amalie," Birch said, and I relented a little, enough to dance with him after the big dinner party at Dovedale.

There was soup with fishballs, pickled pork, ham, sausages, goose liver pie, layered cake with cream and custard, and thickly frosted Vienna pastries. Bavarian beer was served instead of Mor's ale, and most of the men drank too much of it. I never had seen Far so happy, and I seldom did again. The next day, as she had promised, Mor stopped being a hypocrite and made everybody miserable.

She became a regular Berngerd. That is the Danish way of describing a hard woman, and it goes back to the Portuguese Princess Berengaria, who was the second wife of Valdemar the Victorious. Her name, changed to Berngerd in Danish, means "the bear's keeper." Berngerd was noted both for her beauty and for her harshness.

It hurt me to hear the gossips of Ausig call Mor "Herr Shipowner Ormstrup's Berngerd," but as I tried to endure the new austerity at Dovedale, I could see some justice in it.

Each day brought a new harangue about a formerly innocent pleasure. The brew house stood empty and unused, Far's card-playing friends were no longer welcome, and Pastor Madsen was not invited to our table. I doubt that he minded, for the whipped cream cakes were a thing of the past, and the fare was the plainest fish or *frikadeller* and pumpernickel.

The sitting room draperies were pulled aside to mortify Mor's pride in her oriental carpet. The unworldly feet of the "Holy Ones" tracked mud across it, and Mor seemed to take pleasure in its ruin.

Our orthodox friends reacted to her fanaticism by lifting their eyebrows and murmuring, *"Jo ja!"* but Far, Hop-Caroline, and I had to live with her, and we didn't know how to respond to her sharp-tongued preachments.

Mor's constant talk of the love of Christ was strangely coupled with cruelty. At least it seemed cruel to me that she would pour cold water into the soup to prevent our "worldly enjoyment" of it.

from *Petra*

[1]

I WAS BORN IN THE HOUSE on Willow Street just six weeks after my father's death. I can't possibly remember, so I must have been told of the grave faces shadowed by huge hats looming above my crib.

Women came and went, stirring the air with their leg-o'-mutton sleeves, easing their hourglass shapes into chairs, and murmuring, "Poor little thing!" My unfocused infant eyes opened on a world without men.

When I was older, I felt the sorrow Mama exuded like a bitter perfume, but I did not know that mothers were ever otherwise.

Mama held herself straight in plain dresses that indented softly at a waist unpinched by corsets. In the day of the swayback stance, she looked deformed, and I didn't appreciate her timeless beauty until long afterward, when I found Pallas Athena in a library book and shouted, "Here's Mama!"

Knowing her with my eyes was the least of it. As the youngest of five, I shared her feather bed, and I know this memory is mine alone. No one could have told me how the muscle of her forearm rolled under my head, making a suction cup of my ear. I pushed my feet into the springing resilience of her thighs, breathing the sharp-edged sweetness of her skin.

Mostly she turned toward me, careful to breathe above the top of my head. She never squeezed or suffocated, and I felt quite free within the half-moon of her body.

I was her last baby, and she let me cling to her longer than the others had. When I was nearly school age, I was sleeping on her lap during the Danish sermons at the Lutheran church. She never suggested that I was too big to do this; I had to discover it for myself in the scornful glances of other five-year-olds who sat up straight on the hard benches, emulating the stern attention of their elders.

When I started to do the same, Mama told me I didn't have to go to church with her anymore. My older sisters and my brother Stig had been excused from the services long before on the grounds that they didn't understand Danish and would not profit from an hour of wandering thoughts.

Stig welcomed me to a new world of Sunday morning adventures. We pushed our bodies to their limits, which may be one kind of prayer. I could tie Stig in a foot race, so we gave up running for jumping from high places.

On a dazzling October Sunday we crossed the brick street and crept along the Herterts' iron fence, glancing at their house. It was quiet, deserted, which meant the banker and his wife were at a Unitarian meeting in somebody else's house. An odd way to go to church, we thought, but we were glad it wasn't their turn to host the half-dozen families that shared their views.

The rockaway could be seen through the open doors. This meant the Herterts had taken the small buggy, leaving clear the best spot to land when leaping from the loft. We were in luck all the way.

John Hertert's matched bays knew us. They looked up, snorted damp oats from softly ruffled lips, and dipped back into their feedboxes. I scrambled up the loft ladder after Stig, pulling myself dangerously close to the copper-reinforced boots above my head. Just gaining the platform would have been enough for me. Mote-filled sunrays squeezed through cracks in the siding to gild the hay, which prickled pleasantly and smelled mustily sweet. The loft was safe and cozy, a more than ample reward for daring the mild climb.

Not for Stig. His white-blond hair lifted in underwater slow motion as he jumped, and a cloud of dust rose lazily to the spot where he had been.

"Come on," he urged from below, "it's nothing."

He was wrong. I miscalculated and hit a post, raising a huge lump just above my elbow.

"We'd better get home," he said.

"I—I can't walk—"

"Don't be dumb, it's your arm, not your leg." He pulled me up by my good arm. "And don't tell Mama."

The older girls were doing their hair with a curling iron when we got home. The singed smell was so strong in the kitchen that I gagged and vomited in the washbasin.

"You're disgusting," Else said.

Valborg looked at me more kindly and said, "She looks white around the mouth. Where have you two been, Stig?"

He disappeared without answering, and Kamille said, "Hoydens, the two of them! We're just lucky that our characters were formed while Papa was alive."

I threw myself into Mama's feather bed, letting it swallow me and poultice my pain while I thought about Papa. Would he ever be surprised when I got to heaven and told him who I was. He'd go and get my baby brothers and say, "Look who's here! Petra!"

Would it be soon? The throbbing pain in my arm seemed bad enough to get me to Papa.

Mama usually was luminous for about an hour after she got home from church, but the Sunday glow faded the minute she saw my arm.

"If I could pay him, I'd send for Doctor Gus," she said. "This must be God's punishment for letting you run wild. If you had been in church with me, it wouldn't have happened."

"Stig told me to jump and I did it. Why should God blame you?"

"It's my fault."

I couldn't bear it. I cried, clutched her knees, and promised to be good. Danish women control their children by making them feel guilt, and I responded with textbook predictability, but Stig did not.

It seemed that boys could do dangerous things without getting hurt or feeling bad afterwards. Puzzling.

Stig was punished for leading me astray. He could not leave our yard except to go to and from school for two weeks. He acted as if he didn't care, but he blamed me for telling Mama and wouldn't talk to me until I gave him the fish fossil I had found in the bed of the Nishnabotna.

I sighed at the high price of reconciliation, but a pariah who owns a fossil is still a pariah.

Stig and I had to invest our few possessions with magic to give them value, and I looked upon that fossil as God's fingerprint. The older girls had silver hairbrushes, necklaces, and crystal inkwells left over from the unimaginably prosperous days when our father had been a successful general merchant, so they pretended less.

After Papa's death, his partner in the Beehive, Edward Parmeter, cleaned out their joint bank account and ran away to Canada. Else told me about it and warned me never to mention that man's name in Mama's hearing because it made her miserable and flinty-eyed.

I resolved to go to Canada as soon as I was grown to find Edward Parmeter. I would tell him how hard Mama worked, pulling the washing machine lever back and forth until sweat ran down her face, hoisting flatirons from the stove when they sizzled at a moistened finger, nudging the heavy iron noses over the ruching of shirtwaists. Edward Parmeter couldn't know how it was with Mama, or surely he would give back all that belonged to her and restore her to the cool beauty of the Dammand photograph in the parlor in which she wore an ivory silk ball gown and rested a smooth hand on Papa's shoulder. That hand was roughened now by transforming huge wicker baskets of dirty clothes into racks of starched garments that looked like new—and all for fifty cents a basket.

The laundry money and what Mama made selling milk from our cow, Berngerd, at five cents a quart, was our only income. Mama gave her milk customers five cups to the quart, and Stig and I didn't appreciate her generosity. The extra cup added weight to the tin pails we delivered at twilight, causing the bails to cut deep into our palms. Sometimes the shiny, blue-tinged depressions were still visible when we undressed to go to bed.

At least five days of the week were washdays for Mama. She would put the clothes to soak the night before and get up at four in the morning to heat the wash water and shave bars of yellowy-tan lye soap. Our days began in a cloud of soapy steam, with Mama directing our breakfast from the lever of the washing machine.

"No, Valborg, that's the starch pot—the oatmeal is on the back burner."

"Mama," I said, "can I have a big hair bow like Martha Gerber's?"

"When we live on Silk Stocking Street."

"Where's that?"

"It's not a place, Stupid," Else said. "Mama means when we get rich—and that will be never!"

I thought of Martha Gerber and the pink bow four inches across that pulled her sausage curls to the crown of her head. Mama had found a blue bow for me on an old dress of hers, but it was only an inch wide. Worse than nothing! The width of a girl's hair bow measured her father's prosperity. Tears of self-pity collected in my eyes, and I waited until just the right moment to blink, spilling two perfect drops on my cheeks.

"Remember the bonnet," Mama said.

Stig hooted with a mouth full of oatmeal. The matter of the bonnet was funny to him, but it was the most terrible incident of my life.

Lily Hertert, Mama's lady friend across the street, had given me a velvet bonnet with white trim for my birthday. I was born close to Christmas and my presents were marked for both occasions, so to have a special gift on December 29 just because I was born was a wondrous experience.

"Here's something pretty for you, Petra," Mrs. Hertert said as she handed me the crackling tissue paper.

"Lily, you shouldn't," Mama said, even before she saw what the gift was. "Having feeds wanting."

"Beauty ennobles," Lily said with a smile, watching my awed fingers hover above the kitten-soft crimson pile. "Let me tie the strings for you, Petra."

Her fingers were cool and smelled of violets. I was sorry when she took them away, but this freed me to run to the bedroom mirror and gaze at myself in happy disbelief. The halo of white-touched scarlet transformed my skinned-rabbit braids, and for the first time in my life, I was beautiful in my own eyes.

"Tak, tak," I spoke to my reflection in Danish, giving thanks in the language Mama used for her strongest feelings.

Excitement brought the need to urinate, but I could not leave the mirror, and I scissored my legs in the exquisite anguish of postponement until I was forced to make a run for it.

Sitting in the freezing outhouse, I scarcely felt the cold from below. When I had pulled up my drawers, I looked down into the hole, which was dark and faintly steaming. I was seized by the necessity to make my bonnet even more precious. Untying the strings, I held both ends and carefully lowered the scarlet velvet through the opening. The danger of it made me gasp and yet I went further. I let one of the strings go, dropping the brim into shadows that turned it garnet red.

The risk of the single string was delicious, but I was insatiable. I started to swing the bonnet, cautiously at first, then faster until it flew in a blurred circle. The instant the tie slipped from my fingers, I gave a cry that would have been heard in the house had it been summer, but doors and windows were closed against the cold. No one heard me, and I had time to prepare an explanation for my incredible loss. I had taken the bonnet off because my ear itched, and it had fallen in, pushed by the tail of my coat as I turned. That's what I told Mama, and it was all I was capable of telling. A four-year-old knows but cannot express the sacrifice of something precious to a craving for sensation.

Mama concluded that I couldn't be trusted with anything nice, which must have comforted her when she couldn't give me things. I have concurred in her opinion all my life, and I feel uneasy when somebody gives me a beautiful gift, even though I want it with all my heart. Heart? It isn't the heart that wants things. There's a little vacuum just behind the eyes that pulls and sucks at things.

Stig and I discovered that vacuum together, and he shrugged it off, but I grew afraid of it.

In the alley behind our house on Willow Street was an old barn, a new barn, a deserted house, a pigpen, a buggy shed, and a chicken house. These buildings were a private city for the children of the neighborhood, who used them for games and forbidden activities.

The old house had been pulled back from the street to make room for a new one on the Beamis property; its two stories accommodated permanent playhouses belonging to Maud and Ella Drucker, Kamille, Stig, and me.

Kamille had the upstairs room with little green bows all over the wallpaper. Kamille was almost too old for a playhouse, but she came around occasionally to put her things in order. She kept flowers in a chipped vase beneath a sepia picture of a knight with an unearthly light playing on his head. A few books were propped between orangey-red bricks that marked the covers with their fine dust.

My playhouse was the old nursery. We knew it was a nursery because in a corner we found a wooden horse with one leg broken off, and there were marks on the floor where a rocking chair had tilted back and forth. The horse and the fossil were my only possessions, and when Stig claimed the fossil, I had to make up a few things to replace it.

I started off with a throne with a purple velvet seat, adding elegant pieces until that dirty buff room became an incommunicable wonder.

Stig had the parlor downstairs, and he crouched in the blackened hollow of the fireplace to shoot Indians. He kept tadpoles in crocks, and he had put a hair from a horse's tail in a glass of water to watch it turn into an eel. The water grew slimy and the hair remained untransformed. For a while he kept a garter snake in a wooden box to frighten the Drucker girls, but it died for lack of air.

Ella and Maud shared the big dining room. Though there was plenty of room for them to have separate quarters, they decided they could have a grander establishment by pooling their resources.

Ella had a china doll with real hair and arms of soft kid, a tea set of white china, and a miniature brass bed. Maud, who was younger, had a collection of mechanical toys that fascinated Stig: a dancing monkey, a drummer boy, and a fireman that jerked up and down a ladder.

The Drucker girls allowed us to play with their things only if we observed their strict and often silly rules. I could hold the doll named Tilly if I would be the mean aunt from Chicago whom Tilly was supposed to hate. Maud would turn her back while she wound the monkey, the drummer, and the fireman, depriving Stig of his intense desire to see what made them work.

The day Maud and Ella were taken to their grandfather's funeral, we violated the tacit code of the alley community. We trespassed. At first we played with the toys where we found them, but soon I longed to carry Tilly to my nursery, and Stig wanted to set the mechanical toys in motion on the ledge of the parlor mantel. Wanting was doing, and we must have had an hour of pure bliss before we heard Mama ringing the handbell at the back door. It was time to deliver the milk.

An hour of borrowed ownership made the condition seem so real that we didn't think to return the toys to the dining room. Trained to run at the sound of the bell, we sped away, leaving Drucker property in our playhouses.

We didn't think of it again until suppertime, when Mr. Drucker appeared at the front door, wrathful and terrible in his black funeral armband.

"Mrs. Jorgen, your children have stolen my daughters' toys! In our time of grief, I don't see how—"

"Come in, Mr. Drucker, don't shout such things in the street." Mama ushered him into the parlor, took his hat, and rushed to the kitchen to confront us, holding the hat over her heart with a Roman fist.

First a burst of Danish, then a replay in English when she saw we didn't understand. "What is this man saying?" She waved the hat. "Explain to me how the word 'thief' comes into this house. Never, never have we had a thief in this family, and now this man comes here and says—"

"Mama," Stig tugged at her arm, and she threw his hand off violently, "Mama, we didn't steal!"

"It's true, Mama," I said, "we just played with their things and forgot to put them back."

Her fingers crushed the brim of Mr. Drucker's hat. "What is a thief but one who takes a thing and does not give it back?"

"They didn't mean anything wrong, Mama," Valborg said.

"Be still! Stig, Petra, come with me!" She pushed us into the parlor where Mr. Drucker sat, his elbows on his knees, hands covering his eyes.

"Mr. Drucker," Mama said, "I have never been so ashamed! My children took what was not theirs and did not give it back. They will beg your pardon, and then we will go home with you and they will ask the pardon of your daughters." She shoved Stig forward until he nearly fell into Mr. Drucker's lap. "Say it!"

"I—I'm sorry—but we didn't hurt the things, and they can have them back now—"

Mama pulled him away roughly and gave him a stinging slap, then pushed me at Mr. Drucker.

"I'm sorry too, but Ella lets me—"

"Enough," Mama snapped. "Shall we go, Mr. Drucker?"

He rose, looking uncomfortable. "That won't be necessary, Mrs. Jorgen, now I can see how it all happened. I shouldn't have come, but with Papa's passing and the girls crying and carrying on, I just couldn't think—you understand?"

"I only understand that this must be put right—with everyone. Let us go to your daughters."

Mama stood tall, pulling her shawl tight as a bandage, while we told Maud and Ella how sorry we were. The girls were tired and headachy from the funeral and they started to cry. Mrs. Drucker murmured, "Poor little things," and we weren't sure whether she meant us or them.

"Mein Gott!" said Mr. Drucker.

The walk home was a kind of flight. Mama sped along the uneven bricks and we ran behind, silent and scared. At our own door she wheeled to face us.

"Never take anything that does not belong to you! If the wind drops an apple from someone else's tree at your feet, you must not touch it. Nothing can be yours unless you work for it or unless the owner freely gives it to you."

We knew this was the last direct address we would have from her for days. She went inside, abandoning us.

"We had fun though, didn't we, Petra?" Stig said. "It was worth it!"

I shook my head, feeling cold at the thought of Mama's withdrawn approval. It would last forever, according to my measurement of time. Danish rage is slow to kindle, but it smoulders long. Suddenly the doll Tilly was hateful to me, and I wished I had cracked her china face.

Soon afterwards Mr. Drucker bought land in the west and the family moved away. Their house stood empty for a month before the new people came, and it was too securely locked to be any fun.

One day we came home from school to find three wagons pulled close to the door of the Drucker house. The movers carried carved benches, huge brass trays, ivory elephants.

Stig and I were speechless with amazement, but Valborg was bold enough to question one of the men.

"Who's going to live here?"

"A preacher, girlie. Now you'll have to behave."

"Oh, I thought it might be somebody exciting."

"Might be," the man said. "They've been off among the heathen."

"Gol, look at that big sword!" Stig pointed at a wickedly curved blade thrusting out of a coiled basket. "It could cut your head right off!"

I turned to a blur of movement at the door, and there was the most beautiful girl I had ever seen.

"Do be careful with the china barrel," she called.

"Yes, Miss, I'll be careful," said the mover, as smitten as I was by the sweet-toned voice, rich mahogany hair, hand-span waist.

The hair was pulled tight from her forehead and gathered in a lustrous bun and she wore dull blue chambray covered by a rough muslin apron. Anyone else gotten up like that would have been ugly, but she was glorious.

When she saw me gaping at her and smiled hello, I was seized by an agony of shyness and couldn't respond.

"My name is Rachel," she said. "What's yours?"

"P—Petra. I—I live over there."

"Well, Petra, we're going to build a beautiful house of God next to your house, and when it's finished, you must come. Will you?"

I nodded, quite overcome, and ran home. From our side of the fence, I watched Stig leave the wagons and approach my new friend. They talked and talked while I burned with jealousy, and when Stig finally vaulted the pickets to my side, I demanded to know what had been said.

"They haven't got any boys. Nobody but her. Do you know where they've been? In India, where they burn people up when they die—and the cows are holy. She says her Pa tried to teach them different, but it's hard."

"Isn't she beautiful?" I said with a sigh.

"I didn't look at her good. Didn't want to miss any of the stuff going in."

Up to that time I had considered Stig to be an extension of myself, but now I wondered if one or the other of us had been left in a basket on Mama's porch. If he was blind to Rachel's beauty, we couldn't be related by blood.

Soon the workmen came with heavy timbers and brick-laden drays. They dug in the ground to a depth that yielded clay shards and what Stig thought to be an Indian arrowhead.

When the men quit for the day, Stig and I would jump into the hole and pull juicy worms for fishing from its damp walls. Else tried to frighten us away from the hole by likening it to a grave, but this only made the excavation more attractive. Death was a spectacle to us: something that happened to other people, old people like the Drucker girls' grandfather.

After the foundation was set, the walls of the church began to rise. We were forbidden to get in the way, so we sniffed the piney fragrance of fresh-sawn boards and listened to the ring of hammers from behind our own fence, but as soon as the men left, we rushed through our gate for a wild game of hide-and-seek among the piles of bricks and boards.

Crouching behind a wall of rosy-orange bricks, I willed Stig to look for me at the other end of the lot, but I could hear him breathing very close to me. I gauged the short distance between my hiding place and a stack of two-by-fours, shut my eyes, and sprang forward.

"Caught you, Petra," he shouted, and in the same moment I felt the piercing thrust of the nail. I didn't scream until I opened my eyes and saw it—sprouting from my bare foot through a collar of blood.

"You're nailed to the board," Stig gasped.

"Mama!" I screamed, dragging the three-foot length of pine toward our fence, a grotesque shoe.

Mama was milking Berngerd and she came to the door of the shed with the half-full pail in her hand. Seeing my condition, she dropped the pail, slopping the milk in a lacy arc. "Stand still!"

I'd never seen Mama run before, and the sight was more awesome than the blood welling up from my foot. I saw the strong outline of her legs moving beneath the long skirt, the weighted sway of her bosom, and the hands swinging to clutch the air before her.

"Petra, Petra, *lille* Petra!" she gasped, kneeling beside me. "Stig, hold her hands. It will have to come back through the foot."

As the nail retraced its passage, I yelled in pain and terror, and Rachel came running from the parsonage. In her presence I turned stoic, even enjoyed the clean, Castile scent of her hair as she knelt to wrap my foot with the tea towel she carried.

Mama and Rachel made a chair with their arms to get me inside, where Mama readied a cleansing basin of lye soap and hot water.

"Shall I call the doctor, Mrs. Jorgen?" Rachel asked.

"No thank you," said Mama. "I can take care of her."

In a few days, she knew she couldn't. My leg swelled to the size of a telephone pole, erupting yellow pus.

"Dear God!" Doctor Gus exploded when he saw it. "Amalie, why didn't you call me sooner?"

Mama turned away without answering, and then the doctor started to yell at her.

"You and your damned Danish pride!"

Rachel knocked and entered without invitation, rushing to cradle my head on her freshly ironed shirtwaist. "You can't die, Petra, not until you belong to Jesus!"

"Stand back, Miss McLathry," Doctor Gus snapped. "There's no need to talk of dying."

He slathered nasty black salve all over the leg. "Bring two kitchen chairs to put her on, and she'll have to have hot packs every living minute until I tell you otherwise."

For two weeks I lay on the chairs like a small, miserable mummy swaddled in hot, wet sheets. Mama worked on the leg and Rachel worked on my soul.

Much as it pained me, I had to resist Rachel. If I gave my soul to Jesus as she wanted me to, He might take a notion to "call me home," as Rachel put it.

"But Dear," she said with tears in her great, brown eyes, "I'm so afraid for you."

I told her I was sorry, but I couldn't do what she wanted, and when she left, shaking her head and sighing, I told Mama, "I wish I could, but I don't dare."

She gave me a tight smile. "When He wants you, you'll dare. The world is full of people who want others in the fold for their own comfort. Don't let them trouble you."

"But Rachel was just thinking of me."

"Was she?" Mama smiled again and pulled a fresh sheet steaming from the iron pot on the front burner.

When the Evangelical Church was completed, I went to services there, chiefly to hear Rachel sing on Sunday mornings.

Mama never had money to replace anything in the house, but she took good care of what we owned. Every week one room was thoroughly turned out, and spring and fall housecleaning meant scouring, airing, and beating in an atmosphere of ammonia, strong soap, tar paper, and camphor.

Good Friday was the day when the clothes closets were emptied and cleaned because Mama said the sun always shone at least part of that day. We hurried home from school at noon to reacquaint ourselves with all the things stored since fall cleaning day.

Mama had two hats, one for summer and one for winter. The winter hat was a wide-brimmed black beaver with a cockade of jet beads she had worn when Papa was alive, the summer one was gray leghorn straw banded with lilac flowers, given to her by Lily Hertert. They were kept in a big round hatbox with a Beehive label, and beneath their tissue-stuffed crowns was something even more exciting—our family secret.

Papa had given her two twenty-dollar gold pieces the first year the Beehive showed a good profit. Each of us was allowed to hold and admire them twice a year. They glowed like hardened honey.

The gold pieces and Mama's outmoded, elegant dresses kept us from feeling really poor in a time when those who had money and those who didn't were equally obsessed by it.

I was the last to hold the gold pieces, and Mama took them from me, saying, "That's enough until fall cleaning."

At county fair time, we all begged to go, promising not to spend a cent if we could just walk through the dusty exhibit halls to look at prize quilts and jewel-toned preserves, tiptoe behind the giant Clydesdales in the barns, and watch the young men climb a greased pole to win a silver watch.

Mama considered and finally said, "All right, but I'd better come too. The gypsies are in town."

Mama's opinion of the Romanies had worsened since coming to America, she said. The thought of them roaming on the Danish heath had entranced her because she never really saw them and only imagined the good things about them: bright wagons, gay melancholy music, and laughter. Here, they came into full view with their filth and thievery, nudging close to the raw little towns of the Midwest to pillage and gull the unwary.

When we got to the fairgrounds, she marched us close to their encampment in a ragged field north of the grandstand as an object lesson in wrong living.

A blackened pot hung from a tripod above a smudgy cooking fire of green sticks, and a little boy who had just learned to walk tottered naked in the afternoon sun, his brown skin supple and oily-smooth as dressed harness. An old woman with greasy hair escaping a soiled red kerchief and gold loops in her ears pulled him back roughly when he came too near the fire.

Seeing us, the woman reached into layers of skirt and pulled out a pack of cards. "Your future is in my hand."

Mama stiffened and grabbed for Stig and me, signalling to the older girls with a swift toss of her head, "Come!"

"Oh Mama," Else said, "couldn't I please?"

"Don't be foolish! It's all a cheat and a lie."

Else still lingered, staring at the old woman longingly. "If I just knew what was going to happen, maybe I could stand to wait for it."

Mama snorted. "If I had known what I know now when I was your age, I would have jumped into the North Sea. Let's go and look for Mrs. Nicolai's quilt."

We hurried away, but I looked back. The old woman was thrusting the fingers of her right hand at us, and the sight made the hairs rise on my forearms.

While we were looking at prize pickles in the exhibit hall, I told Mama about that fearful hand.

She gasped, "The evil eye!" and told us we'd have to go home.

"Oh, not yet," Valborg protested. "I want to see them catch the greased pig."

I was sorry I'd mentioned the gypsy's gesture, for Mama was determined. Our expedition was over.

We came home to a ransacked house. Drawers hung open, clothes were scattered through the rooms, and the pantry was stripped of flour, sugar, and cornmeal.

Mama ran to her bedroom and gave a wounded cry. At first I thought it was the gray leghorn straw on the bed. She believed a hat on the bed was unlucky. Then I saw the round hat box with one side caved in. The black beaver was gone and so were the gold pieces.

"The gypsies!" she cried.

"I'll get you more gold pieces, Mama," Stig said.

"Your Papa gave me those," she said tonelessly, and that was the last word we ever heard about the gold pieces. We helped her put things where they belonged, and everything looked the same, but we knew it wasn't. We were no longer secretly rich.

Stig said, "If we had let that old woman tell our fortune, we might have known in time to hide things better."

"Dummy," Valborg scoffed. "Do you think she'd tell on her own people?"

"They're no good," Else raged.

"You're the one who wanted your fortune told, Lady Astor," Valborg reminded her.

"Something wonderful is going to happen to me," Else said. "I just know it!"

Else got a job in the fall, but that didn't seem too wonderful. As the Parkers' hired girl, she had to wear a silly little white cap, and Helm Parker grabbed at her every time he caught her in the upstairs hall. I heard her tell Valborg and make her promise not to tell Mama. I hadn't promised, so I told. Mama put on her best dress and walked uptown to Mr. Parker's real estate office to talk to him.

Things went along quietly, boringly, for Else after that—until the Parkers made her pretend to be their niece from Indiana during the weekend visit of a Chicagoan with money to invest in their business.

The Thursday before the visitor was to arrive, Kamille went to work with Else. Kamille was to be the hired girl in Else's place, and Mama didn't know a thing about it. Else cornered Stig and me in the fruit cellar and bribed us not to tell by promising to sneak us into the Parkers' house after school and show us around. Mrs. Parker would be out for the afternoon, listening to Mrs. Boysen deliver a paper on "The Trail of the Saracens in Spain."

Else knew we'd be tempted. The only houses we had entered besides our own were Lily Hertert's and the McLathry parsonage. Stig didn't care about houses, but the idea of sneaking in appealed to him. We started up the long walk to the veranda, expecting to be admitted through the front door with its fancy glass fanlight, but before we reached the steps, Else pulled aside the lace curtains and fiercely directed us to the back entrance.

"This is just like delivering milk," Stig complained.

Else withered him with a glance. "Do you want all the neighbors to see and tell Mrs. Parker that a couple of ragamuffins came to call while she was out? Hurry up, now."

Kamille waved from the pantry where she was polishing silver and said, "Else has me working harder than *she* ever does, I'll bet."

"You're crazy to do it," Stig said.

"But it's so romantic."

Else grasped our upper arms and hustled us from one room to another, urging us to admire, acting as if she owned the place. When we came to the parlor with its three-piece set of green plush, I broke from her to slide on the polished floor.

"If you scratch that floor, I'll kill you! I spent the whole morning rubbing it."

"Don't they have enough money to buy a rug?" I asked.

"Rugs aren't fashionable anymore."

I thought of the ingrain carpet with the big flowers in our seldom-used parlor at home and felt diminished.

The Parkers' bedroom seemed like a church to me. The bed's towering headboard was carved like the pulpit Rachel's father preached from and the wood had the deep glow of pews. Also, the scent of Florida Water, which so many ladies wore to church, was strong in the room.

Else boldly opened the wardrobe and produced a rose-colored dress with high neck and trumpet-shaped skirt. "Mrs. Parker had it cut down for me to wear when *he* comes. Come on, I'll show you where he's going to sleep."

We gazed at the golden oak bed where the important visitor would take his rest. Else smoothed the crocheted bolster cover with a fluttery hand. Her eyes shone, her color was high, and she was so pretty in her excitement that I didn't get mad at her when she shoved us out the back door.

After the momentous weekend, Else was in a glowing trance and we had to get the story from Kamille.

"What did he look like, Kam?"

"Like something Mr. Gibson would draw, but I didn't trust him somehow. He was too slick."

"Did he like Else?"

"He sure seemed to. Leaned all over her when he talked to her and kept saying, 'What's your opinion, Miss Parker?' The Parkers called Else 'Dear' and talked about how popular she was at French Lick. And you should have heard Else saying, 'Yes, Auntie Vera. You're quite right, Uncle Helm.' It was a scream, but I really feel guilty about keeping it from Mama. I'll die if she finds out."

Mama did find out. The rose dress, which Else brought home as some kind of a talisman, gave her away. Mama found it and demanded an explanation. Else was not allowed to return to the Parkers' but she still believed that Mr. Wentz would come looking for her and take her to Chicago, no matter who she was.

Mama apprenticed Else to Mrs. Paup, the best seamstress in town, and Else learned the trade without even thinking about it.

Her fingers seemed to know what to do while she dreamed about Mr. Wentz.

"Else," Mama said, "you can't build your life on a lie. Forget that man."

"I can't, Mama—the way he looked at me—"

"And what were you doing? Oh Else, don't ever give a man a deep look unless you're sure you care for him and he for you—"

"But I *did* care! I do!"

"What about him? If he cared, where is he?"

Else started to cry. She was different after that: cruel. Every day she would herd Stig and me to the fruit cellar for our "daily spanking," which seemed to relieve her feelings. We spent a lot of time hiding from her.

When she met Soren Jensen, Valborg predicted she would change, but Valborg was wrong. Else simply found another victim in this reddish-haired suitor.

Seeing him turn the corner onto Willow Street, flicking his team to a flashy trot, Else would scoff, "Here comes the plowboy."

"Too good for him, are you, Lady Astor?" Valborg said.

"He passes the time."

Soren was a hired man, a Danish immigrant who saved his money and invested it well, inching his way toward financial solidity until he met my sister. He never came to our house without chocolates, hothouse roses, or lace handkerchiefs to give her.

First I pitied him, then I loved him. I had to warn him.

"She laughs at you and gives your presents away."

"No matter—as long as she doesn't tell *me* to go away."

"It's no fun to love somebody who doesn't love back," I said darkly, speaking from the heart.

"She will love me in time."

"No, she'll always love Mr. Wentz."

Soren was visibly alarmed. "Who's he?"

"A man from Chicago who didn't love her back."

Soren looked angry. I had saved him from Else.

But then he said, "What man could be such a fool?" and I knew there was nothing more I could do.

from *The Sailing Out*

[1]

I WAS BORN THE YEAR of the Crash—a few months earlier than Black Friday—but my farmer parents had done their crashing well before their urban neighbors and were well adjusted to the Great Depression by the time I arrived.

After three days of trying to be born in the farmhouse bedroom where my mother was attended by a physician with a powerful yen to go fishing, I yielded to the pull of impatient forceps. That's what gave me the square head that mocked my Aunt Kamille's prediction that I would grow up to look like Queen Marie of Roumania.

My first memories are of lying in the white-painted crib my father had made from banana crates, afraid to close my eyes in the dark. If I lowered my eyelids, the earth opened in great fissures as whirling, shrieking pinwheels came at me. Drugged by the hard work of the day, my parents slept just beyond my reach. The slightest cry would have brought one of them to comfort me, but I lay stiff and silent with my eyes opened so wide that my forehead ached.

As I grew older, another recurring scene was played against the backdrop of heavy, country night. The noon sun lit a rocky grotto where my parents laughed and talked while they spread a picnic cloth and passed food to each other: chicken, coffee with cream, and potato salad covered with slices of hard-boiled eggs that stared with big golden eyes. I ran to join them, but as I came close, the earth split into a deep chasm. Hungry and lonely on the other side, I backed away from the crumbling edges of the deep-cut earth into sleep.

In the morning I looked out the window and marveled that the yard was flat and solid as a table top, packed hard by a flock of pecking chickens, but the terrors of the night stayed with me until I went outside and tested reality with my feet.

When I came into the house, no one questioned my stomping ritual. All was well as the eastern sun poured into the kitchen through the window beside the cookstove. Daddy thanked God for the oatmeal and the scrambled eggs with their tiny green sleeves of chives. My dog Sofus stretched out in a warm square of light on the linoleum, thumping his tail whenever I looked his way. It seemed to me that Sofus particularly appreciated the dress I was wearing, my favorite. I loved the small print of pink tulips so much that I tried to wear the dress inside out when the right side got dirty, but Mom would have none of that. The tulips were clean today, fragrant from the kiss of a flatiron pulled from the stove burners just short of a scorching heat.

Little Bo-Peep in the bottom of my cereal bowl was suffocating in oatmeal, and I ate the stuff to rescue her. She was grateful, and so were her sheep.

Mom was wearing a green headache band and the dress she had made on the sewing machine that said *Bismarck, Bismarck, Bismarck!* when she stepped on the treadle. She looked like a stranger in this new thing, and I squinted my eyes, trying to get her to look the way she always did. I pushed at time to see the dress old and familiar, fading and softening the stiff new material.

She served Daddy's eggs from the big frying pan on a back burner and passed behind his chair to take her own place, touching him as she went. His hand closed on her fingers.

"I know that foxy get-up is for Valborg," he said, "but I'm enjoying it too."

"Well, I don't want her to think I've gone to rack and ruin out here on the farm. Oh, Lauritz, I'm so nervous!"

"That's foolish. She's your sister, isn't she?"

"That's just it. We know exactly how to hurt each other."

"It beats all the way you Jorgen sisters take turns being mad at each other. When a Dane gets a mad on, it's a long, cold winter, and I'm glad the ice is breaking between you and Valborg."

"It's hard to know how to act," Mom said. "The longer a thing like that goes on, the worse it gets. Margaret, please mind me while your Aunt Valborg is here, and be nice to her. You can call her Aunt Val, I guess. That will be easier for you, and Mama says everybody calls her Val nowadays."

I tried to think how Aunt Val would look. Probably like Aunt Kamille, who lived in town. She would have grasshopper green eyes, a straight nose with a little bump at the bridge, and a high twist of molasses-colored hair. Maybe not, though. Mom and Aunt Kamille were as different as the kittens in a barn-cat's litter.

Aunt Val was coming from a place that sounded like the noise the bees made under the eaves of the shed: *Arizona, Arizona!* She was coming on a train, Mom said, and since I'd never seen a train, I supposed it would run on the road like our Ford and bring Aunt Valborg straight down the lane.

"You'd better get started, Lauritz. I'd hate to keep her waiting."

"Won't you change your mind and come to the station?"

Mom hugged her round, white arms. "No, Mama and Kamille will be there, and I'd rather meet her for the first time on my own ground."

"All right—as long as you trust me with a good-looking widow woman."

Mom laughed and walked to the Ford to kiss Daddy good-bye. She always looked away before the car turned out of the lane because she said it was bad luck to watch a loved one out of sight, but I kept my eyes on the square black top until it sank beneath the Fiscus hill.

When Mom went into the house for a knife to cut some Austrian copper roses, I asked for a battered serving spoon to dig in the hard dirt near the back-door pump. The earth was stony, bending the spoon handle against the bowl. Sofus came to help, throwing dirt between his back legs with the furious scrabbling of his paws. When he stopped, looking back at me with his tongue lolling and dripping, I decided his trench was deep enough to bury the picture I had hidden in the back of the buffet drawer.

I was on my way to get it when Mom said, "Margaret, how did you ever get so filthy?" She put the roses on the stoop and swatted the dusty skirt of my dress until the tulips re-emerged, but that wasn't good enough. She said I'd have to change.

"No! I want to wear this!"

"Well, you can't. I won't have you looking like a pig and making Valborg think I let Davy go around like that when he was here."

Davy. He was Mom and Daddy's boy before I came. In the brownish snapshot I meant to bury, they had their arms around him. I had made a hole in his head with a pencil point one wash day when Mom shut me into the dining room to keep me out of the way while she hoisted big kettles of boiling water from the stove to the Maytag. Daddy wasn't with me that day, but when he was, he sat in the big armchair reading *Wallace's Farmer* and listening to the stock reports on the radio. I would climb into his lap and tie his hair into knots that wouldn't hold. When he was tired of such attentions, he would set me down, saying, *"Nuh, suh, lille pige,"* which meant something like "That's enough, little girl."

Sometimes I sneaked down to the barn to be close to Daddy, but he said it was a dangerous place and sent me back to the house. Usually I obeyed, but once I threw a tantrum and refused to go until Jess, the hired man who was in and out of the insane asylum at Clarinda, held out his hand to me and led me away. I loved Jess because he picked up my high chair with me in it and whispered to me. Mom asked me what he said, but I couldn't tell her. Jess did not make words—just sounds that seemed to have colors and mysterious meanings.

When Daddy came back with Aunt Val, Mom ran out to meet them. She had been pulling the tulip dress off over my head when she heard the car. I pulled it back down and followed her. Mom put her arms around Aunt Val, and they both cried. I walked around them twice, trying to get a good look at this aunt who looked nothing like Aunt Kamille, Mom, Grandma, my dead Aunt Else, or the Aunt Laura who lived both far away and in the big album with dark gray pages.

When Aunt Val let Mom go, she grabbed me, and all I could see was the inside of her ear and a curtain of hair as red as the wood of Grandma's cherry buffet when the sun hit it. After the big squeeze, she pulled back, and I saw her twin-peaked mouth of barn-paint red.

"Pretty, pretty, pretty!" she said, lifting me for another hug. "Sweet enough to eat!" She held me so tight that the words vibrated in my chest and stomach. She had a chokingly sweet smell—nasty-nice like the scent of catalpa blooms.

"Valborg," Mom said, "don't spoil her rotten."

"Sorry, Pete, I forgot I was back among the Danes of Iowa—all pinched and proper. They're not like that in the Old Country."

"How do you know? You've never been there."

Daddy had been standing back, just watching, but now he said, "I know because I was born there. You're right, Valborg, we *do* change in America."

Aunt Val winked, and I was fascinated by that quick dip of an eyelid. Nobody else in the family did that.

"Well," she said, "are you going to keep me standing in the yard all day?"

Mom put three coffee cups on the table, but Daddy said he had to change his town clothes for overalls and go to the field.

"Don't work too hard," Aunt Val said, and as soon as he shut the yard gate, she kicked off her shoes and dug into a long, leather pouch decorated with colored beads. "Isn't that the nuts? I was dying for a weed all the way from town, but I just couldn't smoke in front of Lauritz." She lifted a burner from the stove and struck a sulphur match on its rough edge, blowing a shaft of smoke from her red mouth. Cliff Potter our neighbor made cigarettes from loose brown threads and little squares of paper, but Aunt Val's were perfectly round and came from a package.

Mom fanned the air in front of her face. "When did you take up smoking?"

"After John died. It was my way of thumbing my nose at TB."

Mom fussed with her headache band and played with the piping at the neck of her dress. Then she poked at the green diamonds in the goods of her skirt with one finger.

"Out with it, Pete, I know you're dying to ask about Davy."

"All right, how is he?"

"Healthy as a horse, with a negative TB test. You needn't have worried."

"Can you blame me? We loved him like our own."

"It wasn't your business to worry about him. Oh well, I can understand how you would—waiting so darned long for a kid of your own."

Reminded that I was present, Mom told me to go out and play. I chose the west porch, shaded in the late morning and close enough for me to hear the conversation inside. The day was too sunny for my taste. I preferred cloudy weather because all the pictures in my Mother Goose book had the look of a soft, gray day—one without frightening shadows.

"What brought you home, Valborg?" Mom was saying.

"A friend told me about some WPA mural projects. Thought I might have a chance, and now that my nursing career is over, I might as well paint."

"How can you be flippant about John's last illness? It makes you sound so hard."

"These are hard times, honey. Well, I'd better unpack. Do you think Margaret would like to help?"

I scuttled off the porch and got far enough away to come from a convincing distance when I was called.

Aunt Val was to have the south bedroom upstairs. Her scarred leather suitcase bulged with clothes, but I was most interested in a purple dress, peach-colored teddies, amber beads, and bright blue pajamas with a red dragon. Everything had Aunt Val's sweet, heavy smell, which meant they weren't new. Yard goods from the Golden Rule in Grandma's town smelled like medicine and couldn't be used until the store-bought smell was washed away.

Aunt Val dropped the amber beads over my head and marched me to the mirror. "See? Just like the Queen of Sheba." Then she tossed a pile of peach underthings at me and asked me to put them in the drawer. The swollen wood stuck, and she had to help me, saying, "Lots of things take two. Dear God, isn't it the truth?"

She went on rummaging in the suitcase, pulling out a picture I wasn't sure I wanted to see. Still, I didn't want to make her mad, so I looked. There were two boys, but I saw only one, Davy. The body was bigger, but the face was the same.

"He wanted to come with me," she said, "but he's at CCC camp building a park or something. He loves it. I doubt that Davy ever *will* come back here, but then—I thought the same thing about myself when I went away."

I didn't want Davy around, not ever, so I ran around the house three times with Sofus barking beside me. The circling was an obscure act of magic to insure the granting of a wish.

Aunt Val didn't stay as long as she planned, and it was all because of Jess. She found him in her room holding her clothes to his face. When she screamed, he tried to choke her, but I got there in time to stop him. All I did was say his name. He looked like someone just waking up before he went downstairs.

Two men came to take Jess back to Clarinda, and I didn't even get to say good-bye to him. When he started to yell and struggle, Mom took me into the downstairs bedroom and shut the door. In a little while, Aunt Val tapped on the door and came in with her cigarette and the little sauce dish she used for ashes.

"I feel terrible about this, Pete. If I'd just gone away quietly and hadn't said anything—" Aunt Val said. Her fingers moved to the red marks on her throat.

"It's not your fault," Mom said. "With Jess, it was only a matter of time."

Aunt Val sighed. "Well, Kamille's neighbors are driving east tomorrow, and I might as well hitch a ride to Iowa City to find out if my friend's contacts are worth anything. By this time next week, I could be painting the heroic American worker for the eyes of out-of-work Americans in a post office where they can't afford to buy a stamp."

"Couldn't you apply by letter? *I* have a stamp, and living away from home will cost you money."

"Thanks, Pete, but after what happened, this place gives me the creeps."

Aunt Val left the next day in her purple dress with big white dots, but the south bedroom smelled like catalpa blooms for a long time after that. I'd go up there and sit on the bed to think about Jess. People talked about him after church on Sunday mornings. They said he was "funny in the head," "not quite right," "crazy." Whatever he was, I missed him.

When Daddy opened a letter and threw away the envelope with a stamp, I fished it out of the wastebasket. I didn't know how to write the way other people did, but I knew Jess could read the message in my wavy lines: "I wish you would come back. Nobody whispers to me anymore." I put my letter into the envelope and asked Mom to send it to Jess in Clarinda.

She turned her head away from me, biting her lips. Finally she said, "He won't be able to answer your letter, Margaret."

"That's all right, I can't read anyhow." I dredged up a phrase I'd heard somewhere and told her, "I just wanted to drop him a line."

Mom took my letter, but when I saw that it was still on the dining room table two days later, I took it to the mailbox myself. I wasn't tall enough to reach the box and had to go back for my little stool before I could deposit the letter and raise the metal flag.

Satisfied that I had put everything right, I began the endless wait for the return of the hired man.

[2]

We had company for dinner every Sunday in that time when I knew that days had names, suspected that months did, too, but had no conception of years. We raised our own food, and nobody felt guilty about eating it, because we had all we needed and couldn't sell the rest anyhow.

Aunt Kamille and Uncle Karl always showed up on Sundays with Marianne and Jack Russell, the children of my dead Aunt Else. To me, dead meant gone—simply not present—and since I never had known that aunt, I scarcely could miss her.

Daddy let Jack Russell set a line of gopher traps in the fields to get the bounty paid for gopher feet at the county courthouse, and I tagged along to check the traps. I hated it when the gophers were still moving, because then Jack Russell stepped on their heads. It didn't occur to me that he was making them dead—like Aunt Else—because their small bodies were still there, but I knew that he was inflicting pain.

"Don't you feel sorry for them?" I asked.

"No. Why should I? They're pests. Sofus, get away from that trap!" He slapped my dog on the muzzle, and if anyone else had done that, I would have attacked with feet and fists, but Jack Russell could do no wrong. I loved him.

His features were delicate to the point of girlishness, and he never would be a big man, Mom said, but he didn't seem to know that. He was quick to pick a fight, even though he lost them all.

"He'll never amount to anything," Daddy said.

"Now, Lauritz," Mom said, "the poor boy needs a father. Karl does the best he can, but it's hard to raise a boy in town. Maybe we should offer to take him."

I held my breath at the dazzling thought of Jack Russell coming to stay, but Daddy said, "Let him sow his wild oats in somebody else's ground."

Marianne hated the farm as much as her brother loved it. She was musical like her older sister Geraldine. Every Sunday she would say, "I can't believe that you chopped up the organ for firewood. If you hadn't, there would be *something* to do around here." Then she would flounce off to the window seat in the sewing room and stare out, vibrating with boredom until she looked like a pot on the verge of

boiling its lid off. I wanted to see that lid blow, but I dreaded it, too.
"We've got new kittens, Marianne," I ventured. "Want me to show you?"

"No, the excitement might kill me!"

"Marianne," Aunt Kamille scolded, "don't be so nasty to Margaret."

"When do we eat?" said Marianne.

Aunt Kamille sighed and took me on her lap to tell the story of Little Black Sambo. I wondered if running around a tree for a long time would turn *me* into butter, and when we all sat down at the dinner table, I pushed the butter dish far from my plate.

"You set a wonderful table, Petra," Uncle Karl said. "Here's all this wonderful food, and just this morning I caught two kids stealing potatoes out of our garden and eating them raw—mud and all. I darned near got the spade and helped them, but we couldn't spare the spuds."

"Is it really that bad, Karl?"

With a mouthful of scalloped potatoes, he nodded and added a muffled, "Worse."

Aunt Kamille started to choke and had to leave the table. Mom found a square cut from one of Grandma's old tablecloths and wet it at the kitchen pump.

Watching her wring out the cloth until it looked like a white rope, I asked why Aunt Kamille choked and gasped that way.

"It's her old trouble. When she gets upset, the food won't go down. Kam always did bleed for the whole world."

When Mom got Aunt Kam settled on the bed and plastered the wet cloth over her eyes and forehead, I crept into the room to look for the blood, but I couldn't see any.

Aunt Kam lay very still, and the ladies in the picture on the wall above the headboard took no notice of her. They stood there in their white nightgowns as they always did, trailing their fingers along a stone wall and looking at nothing in particular against a sky too blue to believe. I wasn't sure, but I thought their names were Maxfield and Parrish. They weren't much company for Aunt Kam, and I thought that maybe I should stay, but I couldn't. I could hear Marianne excusing herself from the table.

She discouraged my tagging along on her restless wanderings, but she couldn't stop me from stalking her. The kitchen screen door slammed, and I could hear Mom swatting the flies Marianne let in.

Town folks always opened the door too wide.

I used the parlor door where flies were less likely to settle and made it to the windbreak unseen by Marianne. I even got ahead of her, watching the wind make a red-gold flag of her hair and mold her dress tight to her body as I hid behind the sticky trunk of an old pine. She looked a little like Maxfield and Parrish—but crabbier. I could have reached out and touched her as she passed, but I did not dare.

At the stock-watering tank she stopped and ran her fingers along the wet, green fur under the water. I knew just how it felt and smelled—slimy and sort of delicious and awful at the same time. I wasn't supposed to put my hands (or anything else) in the tank, because the livestock didn't like the smell and taste of people, but sometimes I did it. Marianne sniffed at her fingers and wrinkled her nose, wiping her hand on the outside of the tank before she walked on.

At the south pasture she slipped the baling-wire loop off the post, squeezed through without moving the bottom of the gate, and put the wire back. Town folks sometimes forgot, and that was what I was hoping for because I wasn't strong enough to pull the loop off. I could climb the fence, but then I'd be in the open. I risked it, stinging my soles in the jump to the ground. So far, so good.

Marianne walked toward the creek, pulling her shadow behind her. I wanted so much to come close enough to step on that shadow. Running to narrow the distance between us, I whispered, "Don't turn around. Please don't turn around."

She reached the bank of the creek and started down. First her feet disappeared, then her legs and hips. The thought of following her into that deep cut in the earth terrified me. I stopped. When her shoulders and finally her bright hair vanished, I forced myself to the edge to look down. Marianne clung to a small tree growing sideways from the bank to steady herself as she took off her shoes and stockings to wade in the shallow, brown water.

The creek looked so much like my waking nightmares that I scrambled backwards, sending a slide of dirt clods down the incline to bounce off her bare legs. She gave me such a look of rage that I closed my eyes against it, lost my balance, and fell, bringing a heavy section of the bank down with me.

Marianne snatched the back of my dress to keep me from the

water and screamed, "Now look what you've done! How are we going to get back up?"

With dirt in my eyes and mouth and her anger in my ears, I tried to curl up in a ball and wait for the earth to finish swallowing me. This time, I'd have to endure the part of the nightmare that had never happened because I usually fell asleep.

"Oh, get up!" She grabbed my wrist and jerked me to my feet. "You aren't hurt. Take your shoes off because we'll have to walk close to the water until we find a place to climb out."

"I can't. They're tied in knots."

Snorting with exasperation, she knelt to work at the knots while I inspected the pale pink part in her hair and enjoyed the flowery smell of the soap she used. All we had was orange Lifebuoy, and that didn't smell good.

We carried our shoes, walking until our feet were big mudballs that looked like the bottoms of the rotten fenceposts Daddy pulled out of the ground. Every time Marianne found a foothold, it crumbled under her weight. I was glad. As long as we couldn't get out, she couldn't send me away.

"You try," she said. "You're not as heavy."

Wanting to prolong this captive companionship, I told her that I was tired and would have to rest awhile first.

She groaned and sat on a rotted log, dropping her dusty town shoes in her lap. The mud had dried rapidly on our legs, changing their chocolate-dipped look to that of old linoleum. Marianne pulled her skirt high and chipped away the brown crackles with her polished fingernails. The nails weren't long (too much piano playing), but they were pretty. In an over-bold move, I reached out to touch them, and she absently repulsed me.

"Do you think we're still on your farm? Oh, what would *you* know?"

I didn't know, and I didn't care. It was quiet and warm between the deep banks—cozy as a chicken incubator. Quivering blue dragonflies skimmed the brown water, giving me something lovely to look at. It was good, too, that for once, Marianne couldn't run away from me.

She was more restless than ever, though. Poking at a column of bubbles rising from the water, she thrust a stick into the mud and brought up a slimy, brown crawdad. I wanted it, but she threw the thing away in disgust and walked on, ignoring me until she saw the roots of a small tree clawing the air halfway up the bank.

"Come here. When I boost you up, grab those roots and scramble."

She lifted me, hands in my armpits, and I was so overwhelmed by her unaccustomed touch that I simply hung there savoring it.

"Take hold, dummy!"

Her arms trembled with the strain of my weight, and as I caught the roots, their support was gone. I was hanging by my hands.

"Dig your toes in. Pull!"

I did what I was told, uprooting the sapling and falling back on Marianne. She rolled halfway into the water and struggled to her feet, furious.

"Just look at what you've done to me!"

I looked. Creek water had darkened and dulled her hair and the bright flowers of her dress were mud-stained, but I still admired her.

She put her hands to her mouth to yell for help, and I joined in, but when we stopped for breath, there was nothing but thick, Sunday-afternoon silence. The stream moved along sluggishly and the slant of the sun had altered, completely shadowing the water. Soon it would be dark. Pinwheels would scream and whirl before my eyes. My hand crept into Marianne's, and she let it stay there. She shivered in her wet dress.

"We've tried everything else, so I guess we'd better pray. Kneel down."

Cold, slippery mud cupped our knees as we steepled our crusted hands for Marianne's petition. "Dear God, get us out of here!" She wasn't asking, she was telling. When she struggled to her feet, she started to cry.

"What's the matter? Don't you think He will?"

"Someday they'll find our bones," she said with a sob.

I felt the knob of my wrist through the skin and wondered how it would look when somebody found it. Like the rabbit bones Sofus found in the timber, I supposed.

Marianne touched her lips with the tips of her fingers and sobbed even harder. "All wasted!"

I threw a stick into the creek and watched it move slowly on the water. If the stick stayed in the middle of the stream until it was out of sight, it would mean that someone would come for us right away. When the stick drifted to the far bank, I changed the rules because I was really ready to go home. The banks seemed higher now, and the cut between them was filling with cold, bluish-tan twilight. Mom would be touching a match to the wick of the kerosene lamp in the kitchen.

Marianne decided that we should have gone the other way, and we started back, walking in our own footprints. The only sound was her sniffling and the sucking noise as we pulled our feet from the mud. Once I thought I heard someone calling my name, but Marianne couldn't hear it. She told me this was no time to get funny.

Then she heard it, too. We tried to answer, but we were too hoarse to make much noise. Fortunately, she could whistle. Sofus soon was above us, his golden coat blazing in the late sun that couldn't reach us. He almost stood on his head scrambling down the steep bank to jump and whine and lick our faces. I hugged him, drawing comfort from his sun-warmed coat, and even Marianne, who never liked him, said, "Good dog! Good boy!"

Daddy and Uncle Karl followed the dog, asking if we were all right and thanking God. Jack Russell was there, too, and he yelled at Marianne, "You're lucky the kid's O.K. If anything happened to her, Aunt Petra would have your hide! You could have got out, you dope! Why didn't you make a run for it and take that bank like a fly on a wall?"

"Just come down here and try it yourself, smart aleck!"

Jack Russell flopped on his belly and the men held him by the ankles, lowering him until he could reach our hands. They pulled me up first, then rescued Marianne.

Daddy buttoned me inside his overall jacket and carried me. Half-hypnotized by the even jar of his long steps, I looked over his shoulder at the creek with a feeling of triumph. It had tried to swallow me but failed.

Mom was lighting the lamp in the kitchen. She blew out the long wooden match, turned the wick up to make a fat orange tongue of flame, and hugged me hard, mud and all.

Aunt Kam sat in the kitchen chair beside the cob basket looking pale and stern. She told Marianne to clean herself up as well as she could and they'd go home.

"No, Kam," Mom said, "please stay for supper."

"If we expect to get any, we'd better," Jack Russell said, and they stayed, but Aunt Kam choked again and couldn't eat anything.

Marianne put on one of Mom's dresses, so big on her that it

looked like a gunny sack tied with a rope. She didn't talk at all, but she ate: three pieces of cold chicken, lots of potato salad, and a big piece of burnt-sugar cake with two glasses of the milk she usually refused to touch because it was "right out of the cow." She didn't want to go home until it was good and dark because she didn't want to be seen in Mom's dress.

When they did go, Daddy carried me out to their car in my pajamas to say good-bye. Leaning from his arms, I tested what I supposed to be a new relationship with Marianne by touching her wrist through the open window.

"You get to take your bones home, Marianne," I said.

She pulled away and wouldn't look at me.

"Don't be such a snot, Marianne," Jack Russell told her, leaning across her lap to tickle me. "So long, Snooks."

Exhausted but fighting sleep, I begged to stay up, but I landed in bed. When my eyelids dropped of their own weight, I held my breath in the familiar terror of anticipation. The soft, black void caught me by surprise—no fissures, no whirling pinwheels—just slow exhalation and sleep.

[3]

Grandma lived alone in a dark blue house in Harlan, and when anyone needed her, she came and stayed for as long as her houseplants could get along without her. Before Mom and Daddy went to the stockyards in Omaha to sell cattle, they brought her to the farm to stay with me.

"What was your name when you were little?" I asked her.

"Amalie, the same as it is now."

"Nobody calls you that. You're either Mama or Grandma."

"That's so. I guess I'm the only one who really knows who I am, and sometimes *I* forget."

Grandma wore her dresses to her ankles and covered her skirts with long aprons tied at the waist. Her hair was gray with yellow streaks, twisted into a high knot held with a tortoise-shell comb. She smelled like growing things in the garden, and her hands were spotted with brown.

I found out how hard those hands could be. Mom always let me play in the flour when she baked, but when I poured out my small white mountain while Grandma was stirring dough, she shook her head and scooped it back into the cannister. It was also my custom to grab one of the long, black breadpans before they were greased for a "ride in the Ford" on the linoleum, but when I did that, she tumbled me out and gave me a good swat. I was too surprised to yell.

By the time the bread was set to rise, giving off a yeasty fragrance from the top of the warming ovens, we were friends again. Grandma showed me the dances of the Old Country, lifting her skirts to display footwork that seemed too flashy for tan-lisle ankles and tightly laced oxfords. She told me about keeping the sheep on the moors, and I imagined her carrying a crook prettied up with a blue ribbon like the one carried by Little Bo-Peep in my oatmeal bowl. When I asked her if hers had a bow, she just laughed.

"It's time to gather eggs," she said. "Take the brown pan."

Collecting the eggs was an adventure. The easiest way to do it was to yell and clap, putting the hens to squawking flight, but Mom didn't like me to treat her hens that way. I had learned to reach a sly hand under an angrily-puffed breast, grasp a warm oval, and get out fast. If my timing was off, a sharp beak raised a bead of blood on my hand, but that only happened when I allowed myself to be distracted by the menacing clucking. I was looking forward to the day when my hand would be big enough to grab two eggs at a time, cutting the occasions of risk in half.

I hated the nasty, feathery smell of the henhouse, and I tried to make one deep breath of fresh air last as long as possible. It never worked, because I had to pause to let my eyes adjust to the dimmer light. It was important to see well enough to avoid the snails of chicken filth on the floor. I could hold my breath only so long, and I had to choose between smelling it and stepping in it.

I filled the brown pan without getting pecked, but the hens were really letting me have it in chicken language. As I started back to the house, I saw Grandma smiling at me through the kitchen window. I waved, indicating that I'd be in as soon as I visited the backhouse.

This functional shack stood near the windbreak of pines. The wind made sad sounds in the trees as I edged onto the small hole cut especially for me between two larger ones. The edges of the big holes were worn smooth, but mine was too new for comfort. To make myself forget the biting pressure, I dropped an egg down the hole beside me and listened as it broke with a dull, "plocking" sound far below. I tried one in the other hole, and the sound was slightly different. By the time I had made use of a page of saws and hammers from a Montgomery Ward catalog, the brown pan was empty.

Knowing that Grandma would be mad because she was waiting for the eggs to make a cake, I went back to the henhouse to urge the biddies to lay more, but they slid the membranes across their mean-looking eyes and ignored me. I clapped my hands to scare them off the nests, but the straw hollows were empty. I choked in the feather-filled dust, realizing that I was in real trouble.

Sure enough, Grandma was knocking on the windowpane with her wedding ring, reminding me that she was waiting. I walked slowly to the house with the empty pan behind my back.

"Well, where are the eggs?"

"They aren't laid yet."

"What? I saw you carrying a full pan to the backhouse."

So she had. I cast about for another explanation. "Sofus knocked me down and broke them." As I spoke, I realized that my entire route was visible from the window.

"I don't see any shells," Grandma said ominously. "Let's try once more."

"A big snake came into the backhouse and swallowed them—every one of them!"

"Margaret, come here."

Grandma's hands moved quickly to her apron pocket, and I saw a small glint of gold. I stood before her, interested and a little scared.

"Stick out your tongue."

My impulse was to clench my teeth, but I didn't have the will to go against her. I did what I was told and felt a painful prick. I couldn't believe what had happened to me until she brought the tiny, gold safety pin between her thumb and forefinger close to my eyes.

"See? This is what happens to tongues that tell lies. Remember it."

I was too shocked to cry. Hiding under the kitchen table with Sofus, I tried to decide whether I was mad at Grandma or not. Mom would have taken me on her lap and told me how disappointed she was that I hadn't told the truth, and I would have climbed down with a gnawing feeling of guilt. Now, as I sucked a salty pinpoint of blood, I had a different feeling. I had paid for my lies, and I didn't have to think about them anymore. The relief was like that of the moment when pain stops, and I felt the full joy of it when Grandma's hand reached under the table to offer me a tiny ball of pie crust dough.

"Since we can't have cake, it will have to be pie," she said, and I watched the full bell of her gray plaid skirt swing energetically as she used the rolling pin on the table above me. The air was clear between us.

Grandma also came to us every Christmas and stayed for a week. One morning I woke early to dull, gray light and found myself in the unfamiliar softness of my parents' featherbed. While I was trying to understand why I was there, Grandma lifted her night-capped head from the other pillow.

"Goddag, lille pige."

Sometimes she spoke to me in Danish, which I didn't understand, but I knew that this short greeting amounted to "Good morning, little girl." I asked where Mom and Daddy were and why we were in their bed.

"I came in to keep you from waking up alone, and then I decided we might as well keep each other warm."

"But where did they go?"

"To town. Jack Russell had an accident—the Studebaker skidded on the ice and hit another car."

"Did he get hurt?"

"Not much, but Vivian Corley was killed."

I pondered that information and felt a nasty thrill that I had no intention of sharing with Grandma. Jack Russell had brought Vivian Corley to see us once. Her dark brown hair was in finger waves, and she had a dent in her cheek when she smiled. When anyone talked to her, she answered without taking her eyes from Jack Russell's face. When I stepped between them to block her view, she leaned half off her chair to see around me.

"How do you like my girl?" Jack Russell asked me.

"I'm your girl," I said, and everyone laughed—even Vivian Corley. I glared at her, pretending my eyes were magnifying glasses to catch the sun and burn holes in her, rather than in paper. I concentrated on the burning so hard that I saw the pattern of the parlor wallpaper through a hole in her forehead just below the dip of a finger wave.

Our telephone ring, two longs and a short, shrilled and brought me back to the present. Grandma jumped out of bed to answer, leaving me alone and terrified. Vivian Corley seemed to walk toward me with a hole in her forehead. I moaned, diving under the covers, but new terrors awaited me in the darkness there. The cracks in the earth, missing since my creek-bed adventure with Marianne, were back in full force.

When Grandma came back to bed, she misunderstood my suffering and tried to reassure me. "Don't cry, Margrethe." She said my name in the Danish way. "Jack Russell only broke his arm."

We went to town the day of the funeral, and I begged to see Vivian, but they wouldn't let me. I'd never know whether I'd really burned a hole in her forehead.

During the services I was to stay with Marianne at Aunt Kam's house, a rare privilege I couldn't appreciate under the circumstances. While everyone was getting organized to go, Jack Russell clung to the colonnade between the dining room and the parlor with his good arm. His broken arm looked like a big plaster chicken wing until Uncle Karl hid the sling under a shirt and the dark goods of Jack Russell's best suit.

Aunt Kam tied his necktie, saying, "I think it would be a kindness to the Corleys if you stayed home."

"I have to be with her as long as I can."

Aunt Kam sighed and helped him into his overcoat. Her eyes were the yellow-green of a dying plant, the color they took on when she was troubled. In happier times they were greener.

Jack Russell went down the walk like an old man, supported by Daddy and Uncle Karl. Mom and Aunt Kam followed, picking lint from each other's dark coats. They would stop for Grandma on the way to the funeral parlor. The worst thing, they said, was having to drive the fatal Studebaker.

When they were gone, Marianne went to the piano and played something loud. When she was tired of that, she talked, but *not to me.*

"Vivian wanted a navy blue dress the worst way, but her folks said young girls should wear color. Mrs. Schack from the funeral parlor went to Fern's Fashion and bought the dress Vivian wanted. It had a white lace collar, and I was crazy about it."

"Does she have that dress on now?"

Marianne glared at me. "Of course, you imbecile, that's why Mrs. Schack bought it."

"Did you see her?"

She whirled and grabbed my shoulders, sinking her nails. "You morbid, little monster! I don't even want to *think* about death. I only know about the dress because everybody at school was talking about it."

"I'm never going to get dead," I said, ducking out of her painful grasp.

"That's what *you* think! You'd better get out of my sight before I rub you out personally."

"What does that mean?"

She gave a snarling imitation of what she said was "George Raft and Edward G. Robinson mixed together." I didn't know who they were and didn't dare to ask.

Leaving Marianne in the parlor, I headed for the dining room to look for Punkin, Aunt Kam's sixteen-year-old tomcat. He was asleep in the window seat, and when I touched the furry frown between his ears, he stiffened and made a noise like a storm blowing up.

"Leave that cat alone!" Marianne yelled.

I would in a minute, I thought, but not until I pulled his tail to let him know what I thought of his attitude toward me. He yowled, raking my forearm. The dull, old claws made a triple trail of blood that called for further retaliation. I snatched up a doorstop shaped like a dog and brought it down on his paw. When he screeched and fled, leaving a snowfall of white and yellow hair in the block of sunlight he had vacated, Marianne snatched the doorstop from me and twisted my arm.

"What are you trying to do, kill him? Here Punkin, here kitty, where are you, angel boy?"

Punkin answered from the kitchen in his cracked, old voice, and she ran to him. I could hear her cooing and making kissing noises, and when she came back with the sagging, shedding cat in her arms, she said, "Aren't you ashamed to hurt this poor, old thing?"

"Yes, but he hurt me first." I showed her my arm. "Now we're even." If she had shown any interest at all, I could have explained that I dealt with a bump from a piece of furniture in the same way. I kicked it back, and that was that.

Aunt Kam kept a stack of *National Geographics* on the bottom shelf of the library table, and I became so engrossed in pictures of the

Sphinx and the Pyramids that I gave Marianne no more trouble.

When they came home from the funeral, Mom asked if I had been a good girl. Marianne rolled her eyes and went to her pink and green bedroom, shutting the door with a bang. I yearned to go into that room and look around, but I never dared.

I looked out the front window and asked, "Why is Jack Russell standing out on the porch?"

"He wants to be alone," Aunt Kam said.

Mom said, "Maybe you should have let him stay at the cemetery."

"What would people think? It's bad enough already—everyone poking each other and whispering—you'd think he was a murderer or something."

Uncle Karl sighed. "I guess that's what the Corleys *must* think. Maybe they have a right. Jack Russell drives like a lunatic. I only gave him the car keys because I remembered what it felt like to be too young and poor to own a team and buggy when I wanted to go courting."

"What's a murderer?" I asked.

"Shhh!" Mom said.

Daddy explained, as he always did. "A murderer is a person who kills another person."

"Oh," I said, "then Jack Russell isn't one."

"Out of the mouths of babes!" Aunt Kam said, and they all started to talk about something else before I could finish what I was going to say. I was the murderer. I was the one who burned a hole in Vivian's forehead shortly before she was dead. I could see that they didn't want to hear about that, so I put on my coat, hat, and mittens and went out on the porch. Jack Russell was sitting on the rail, trying to strike a match with one hand. The hand shook.

"Hold the book for me while I strike it," he said.

I took off my mitten in the hope of touching him. Until the match flared, our flesh was joined, and his face came close to mine when he bowed to light his cigarette.

"You've still got me," I said.

Jack Russell choked, threw the cigarette into the snow, and put his hand over his face.

"Was her dress nice?"

He groaned, turning away from me, and I grabbed at the empty sleeve, trying to bring him back.

"Jack Russell, please tell me—was there a hole in her forehead?"

"Oh God!" he blurted, then leaned over the rail to throw up on the snow.

[4]

As the winter wore on, we settled into a lulling routine bounded by morning and evening chores. Daddy was in the house more, reading and writing figures in a book with lines. Sometimes he read to me, and I tried to match words I could hear with marks I could see.

I asked Mom to read "Goldilocks and the Three Bears" and "The Little Match Girl" until I memorized enough to believe that I was reading with her, but sooner or later, we got to the point where I had to drop out and listen.

When nobody had time to read with me, I made squiggly lines on paper, usually the back of a calendar month that had passed, and called it a story. When I could sneak Sofus into the house, I read my stories to him, but he was a farm dog, and Daddy thought it would ruin him if he spent time indoors.

The parlor and the upstairs rooms were shut in winter. We were together in a small space that had the closed-in smell of cobs for starting the kitchen stove, kerosene for the lamps, onions for the Danish meatballs called *frikadeller,* orange Lifebuoy, and manure on barnyard boots.

The downstairs bedroom was warmed by the dining room wood stove only at night. When Mom opened the door a few hours before bedtime, it had its own smell: feather pillows, a whisper of 4711 from Mom's handkerchief drawer, and a faint reminder of the white enamel chamber pot that spared us dark, cold trips in the night. Maxfield and Parrish couldn't smell anything. Their perfect noses remained unwrinkled behind the glass that locked them into their own world of bluest skies and palest stone.

A visit from the Watkins salesman was a big occasion for us. Mom said she couldn't afford to buy much, but she always tried to make some small selection from his case of bottles and boxes to insure a return visit. When the Watkins man hit the neighborhood, the word went out on the party line, and she checked her cupboards.

"Vanilla, maybe?"

"Petra, you have three bottles on the shelf," my dad pointed out.

"Well, I can always use vanilla."

The Watkins man must have had a name, but nobody ever used it. His black Ford was exactly like everyone else's, but it seemed to have a special shine when it came down the lane. The Watkins man climbed down, reached inside for his case, and took a quick look around to locate the dog before he walked to the welcome he was sure to get.

Mom let him show her everything before she said, "I guess I could use a bottle of vanilla."

"You must bake up a storm, Mrs. Langelund. I seem to remember selling you a bottle the last time I was here."

Mom turned pink and said nothing. We watched him rummage in the case for the vanilla, then hesitate and put his hand on something else.

"Tell you what I'm gonna do." He pointed at me. "This young lady here deserves the best, isn't that so?"

"That's so."

"Now, Mrs. Langelund, I know you're a good cook and a good mother, but scientific ree-search has figgered out that three squares a day might not be all we need to stay healthy. I realize that you know me as the Watkins man, but I have two or three items from other companies besides. You want this young lady to be as healthy as possible, don't you?"

"Of course I do."

"Then let me tell you about these capsules that spark the appetite, build up the blood, and keep that old body motor runnin' smooth."

The capsules were long and green—shiny in their gelatin casings—and Mom was afraid I couldn't get one down. She said they looked like horse pills.

The Watkins man laughed and said she was mighty sharp to say so because they contained a compound of pure alfalfa and a secret ingredient. He was willing to bet money I could swallow one, offering it to me in the palm of his hand. I got it down, and Mom bought a box.

A few days later, I took a handful of the pills outside, pulled the capsules apart, and poured the green powder down the tongue of my coaster wagon. It sure did smell like alfalfa.

Mom was on her way to the henhouse when she saw the pile of green powder on the ground. She let out a shriek. "Margaret, what have you done? Those pills cost a lot of money."

I explained. "The Watkins man said they would keep the motor running smooth."

"But your wagon doesn't *have* a motor."

"Neither do I," I said, mildly surprised that she had so much trouble understanding me.

"All that money down a wagon tongue," she said with a groan. "I should spank you."

From her tone I knew she wouldn't, but when she went to her hens, I sat in the wagon and wondered about the stuff called money. Once in a great while, someone gave me a penny. That was money, but I didn't get too excited about the brownish bits with faces on them. Pennies were no more interesting to me than the suckers with wooden handles the storekeeper gave me when we bought groceries in Fiscus. The suckers never tasted as good as they looked, so I left them in their cellophane, sticking them into a cup until I had a bouquet.

One of the high points of my week was the arrival of the *Des Moines Sunday Register.* It was rolled tight and banded with brown paper that had to be slit with a paring knife. The sharp smell of ink filled the kitchen as Mom pulled out the colored comics and gave them to me. When the rest of the paper had been read, Mom used it to start fires in the stoves, but she never touched a match to the comics. They were mine to be kept in a stack and enjoyed forever.

One April Friday I came upon a real treasure, an "Andy Gump" that had been used to line the silver drawer. It had been covered over with a drab black and white page that I tore when I was putting forks away. I eased it out carefully to keep Andy and his friends in one piece.

I found Mom dusting and pinching dead leaves from the potted fern. I didn't think that she'd stop and read to me, but when I asked, she shoved the dead leaves into her apron pocket and sat down.

"It's such a heavy day that I just can't make myself work."

I loved the clear, gray light with no shadows under a soft, pressing sky. Morning and afternoon were all the same, and change did not threaten. "Andy Gump", whose mouth was down in his neck, and Min, whose nose looked marvelously pinchable, lived in a place where every day was exactly like this.

"Oh, Min!" Mom read to me. It didn't sound quite right. She tried again and did better. I never heard what came next, because a voice from outside was yelling Mom's name.

"That sounds like Cliff Potter," she said, dropping the funnies to go out and see what he wanted.

I stayed in the big chair, trying to puzzle out the words in the balloons above the heads of Andy and Min. Mom had turned on the radio when we sat.

It had warmed up enough to deliver a musical phrase that filled me with melancholy, some men singing, "driftin' along with the tumblin' tumbleweed." I wasn't allowed to touch the radio knobs. The only way to escape the song was to leave.

I grabbed a sweater and started outside, shoving one arm into a sleeve as the kitchen door banged behind me. The other sleeve dangled, forgotten, as I stopped and stared.

Mom seemed to be struggling with Cliff at the gate. She was crying. Then Anna, Cliff's wife, came running down the lane. That was something to see. She was a big, fat woman, and she was moving fast with her arms wide open. Just before Anna got to the gate, Mom broke away from Cliff and ran toward the windbreak.

"Mom," I yelled, "wait for me!"

She didn't seem to hear me, and when I tried to open the gate to follow her, Cliff yelled at me to get back. The yard was filling with cars screeching to stops. Men got out of them and ran to the field. I wanted Sofus, but he didn't come when I called. Nobody paid any attention to me. They were pointing at a thin finger of smoke rising from the creek where the bridge was. I couldn't see the bridge for all the men standing around, but when some of them clambered down the bank, I spotted Sofus's golden coat. He was lying there, looking down.

I finally got the gate open and started to run toward the creek, but the preacher caught me and carried me back to the house. I kicked and begged to be put down, but he paid no attention. He was making his Sunday sounds: "Oh Lord, show Thy mercy in this hour of grief." He put me over the top of the fence without bothering with the gate and went toward the trees where Mom was. Dr. Gus from town ran after him. Then Anna Potter took me inside and gave me a red sucker I didn't want. I was adding it to my bouquet when Dr. Gus and the preacher brought Mom into the house. She was quiet now and she didn't seem to hear anything. They put her to bed, but it wasn't night.

When Grandma came, all the strange people went away. She fixed me a bowl of bread and milk and told me to be quiet because Mom was sleeping.

"Will you finish reading 'Andy Gump' to me?"

She started, but then she said she didn't have the heart.

"Aren't you going to fix supper for Daddy?"

"No, Margaret. Your daddy doesn't need any supper here because God has taken him home. Get ready for bed, and I'll hear your prayers."

I started to protest, but thought better of it. I thought while I was putting on my pajamas, and when I knelt beside the bed in the upstairs room I would share with Grandma that night, I said, "God, send Daddy back!"

"You mustn't ask that."

"Why not? That's what I want, and He'd better do it, too."

Grandma sighed and told me that nobody bossed God around. She decided to come to bed, too, even if it was too early for big people to go to sleep. I escaped the terrors of the dark in her arms.

The next day Mom was up and walking around, but she didn't seem to be awake. Uncle Karl came to drive us to town, but I did not want to go because I thought Daddy might come back while we were away. The green Studebaker Jack Russell had wrecked still moved, but it looked like a tin can stepped on by a horse. Uncle Karl made me get into it.

In town we stopped at a big house where the lights were held up by ladies that looked like Maxfield and Parrish. Even though the sun was shining, the lights were on under shades that gave the room a blue-green look. Flowers that looked as stiff as wheel spokes in their baskets were everywhere. They smelled cold.

A lady came to meet us and whispered to Mom. When she pointed to a long hall, Grandma took my hand and said, "I'll take her, Petra."

The hall seemed to go on forever. I asked, "Does God live here?"

"Yes and no. Come."

I certainly was surprised to see Daddy lying in a bed with a pink spread pulled to the middle button of his church suit. Obviously God hadn't understood me. I had told Him to bring Daddy back to the farm, but he'd made a mistake.

"Can I wake him up?"

"No, Margaret." Grandma closed her eyes for a minute and pinched her lips together hard.

Then we went back to Mom, and the whispering lady gave me a sucker—a green one. I thought about how I'd have to straighten this business out when I talked to God again at bedtime.

We had supper at Aunt Kamille's. Marianne invited me into her pink and green room for the first time ever and let me play with her jewelry while the women were doing the dishes. She even gave me a small compact filled with Lady Esther powder. The lady on the top of it wore a blue dress and had white curls piled high on her head.

"I'm sorry about your dad," Marianne said. "I always liked Uncle Lauritz."

"I'll get him back."

"What? What did you say?"

"I'll get him back. I asked God, and He sent him to the wrong place, but when I—"

"Margaret, hasn't anybody told you what this is all about? Your dad is dead—dead like Vivian Corley."

"No! I already saw him sleeping."

I threw the alluring compact on the bed, rejecting gift and giver, and it was a long time before I would believe that Marianne was right.

[5]

When Daddy didn't come back to do his work, Mom put on overalls and went to the field. Somebody had to take care of me, so Grandma locked her blue house on Willow Street with a skeleton key and came to the farm to live with us.

Mom taught herself to drive the Ford. Starting it was easy. She turned the crank and jumped in to take the wheel, but when she had circled the barns and the corncrib until she was dizzy, she couldn't make it stop. She shut her eyes and ran the car into the haystack, where it chugged away until Cliff Potter could get there to turn it off. After that, she could drive. I wasn't thrilled with that development because I always got carsick after riding much more than a mile—more so when I smelled the gas she bought from the single pump owned by the Olsen Brothers Trucking Company in Fiscus. The top of the pump resembled a jar of orange pop. Each time I saw it, I marveled that it could look so good and smell so bad.

Daddy left before the corn was planted. Mom wasn't sure she could do that, so the hired men came, one after another. I was hoping for one as nice as Jess, but I always was disappointed. The first hired man was dark and hairy, somebody from far away. He grabbed Mom in the barn and tried to kiss her. I saw it from the hayloft, where I was playing with a new litter of kittens. Mom spat in the straw and scrubbed her mouth with the back of her hand. That surprised me, because when I tried to spit the way men did, she told me ladies didn't do that.

"Aw, c'mon, Miz Langelund, you're too much woman to go to waste."

"I had a man," she said, "and he was man enough to last me all my life. Put your things together and get off the place. I don't want to look at you again."

"Guess it's true what they say about Dane women—they'll freeze your balls off!"

Mom seized the pitchfork, and he backed toward the door.

"Now don't get excited, I'm goin'—I'm goin'."

Once outside he didn't move very fast. I watched him through a wide crack in the barn boards. When he got to the hog house, he turned around and touched two fingers to the bill of his greasy cap. Then he jabbed his middle finger at the sky and headed for the house. Below, Mom was leaning against a manger with her shoulders shaking. I heard her say, "Oh, Lauritz, I *do* need you."

Another of the hired men had a shiny, bald head that turned pink as a slice of ham when he was out in the sun. Mom finally gave him Daddy's old hat to wear. One hot July noon he was sleeping under the trees with his mouth open, crumbs from his dinner caught in the stubble of his beard. I couldn't resist tickling the washboard roof of his mouth with a foxtail weed. He woke with a roar, broke a switch from the spirea bush, and laid into me.

Mom saw the whole thing from the window and sent him away.

I was glad to let her deal with him, because I no longer had confidence in my own magic—the small rituals I'd been trying since God disappointed me about bringing Daddy back. I'd done everything from touching fence pickets in a special order to burying and resurrecting box elder bugs, but nothing helped.

Daddy was under a mound of dirt in the Harlan cemetery next to Aunt Else and Uncle Soren. We went there to pull weeds and plant flowers on the graves. Daddy's was a brown hill, but the others were flat like gardens. Mom's daddy was buried under a big, old pine that he had planted himself when it was small enough for him to carry on his shoulder with its roots in a gunny sack.

"He's in that tree now," Grandma said, but I never could see him. When I backed away for a better view, Mom told me to watch out for the poison ivy that laced the hedge with glossy green.

After that long summer of many hired men, Mom walked me to the one-room school taught by Miss Eleanor Olsen. I carried a new metal lunchbox that made me proud.

"Take a good look around you so you'll remember the way," she said. "Tomorrow you'll go alone."

We passed the Potters' farm, and Anna waved from the window. At the Denkmans' corner we turned south. Clifford Denkman had helped Mom with the field work between hired men. I liked him and his jolly, messy wife, Ruby, but their son Virgil was, as Grandma put it, "another kettle of fish." As far as I knew, Virgil was incapable of speech. At church suppers he loaded his plate and took it to a corner, turning his back on everyone while he ate so fiercely that I was reminded of the Angus bull that tossed its head, pawed, and snorted when anyone approached its pen.

I was hoping that Virgil wouldn't be at my school, but Mom told me he would.

"This is his last year. Just keep out of his way."

Between the Denkmans' corner and the school was the Larson farm with an inviting lane that poured downward from the road to an arched gate laced with morning-glories of eye-stabbing blue. I could imagine Shirley Larson moving comfortably around the kitchen of that square, white house. She was one of my favorite church ladies; the Shirley who, with Goodness and Mercy, would follow me all the days of my life.

As we came to the schoolyard, my stomach tightened. I'd never seen so many kids running and yelling in one place. I knew some of them from Sunday school, but we exchanged no sign on this new ground.

I also knew Eleanor the teacher, but Mom told me I'd have to call her Miss Olsen now. I wasn't sure I could remember that until I saw her come out of the school with a bell in her hand. Her hair was finger-waved, and her body looked like a vase in a dark plaid dress. She was no longer Eleanor, who wore overalls to help her trucker brothers load oats. This stranger was Miss Olsen the school teacher.

Mom disappeared without saying good-bye, and Miss Olsen said she'd show me my desk. I slid into the smooth, dipping seat and ran my fingers over the curly, iron grillwork at the sides. I couldn't read the words cut into the desk top and blackened with pencil lead, but I was confident that I would be able to read anything by the end of the day. That was what I had come to learn.

I was disappointed that I still couldn't read by the time Miss Olsen rang the hand bell and said, "Recess, people," but I wasn't surprised. She didn't stay with us long enough to show us how to do it. She wrote "A, B, C" on the blackboard, and told us to learn that much while she worked with the bigger kids. When I said, "A, B, C, D," she gave me a funny look and said I had to put up my hand when I wanted to talk.

I stood aside when everyone rushed to the door for recess, winding up last in line for the swings and teeter-totter. Next time I'd know better. While I waited for my turn, I watched Virgil Denkman climb the pole to the top of the swing frame and hold the chains, keeping the kids in the swings from pumping high.

"Virgil," Miss Olsen said, "get down from there this minute."

"You gonna' make me?"

I listened, amazed. It wasn't Virgil's surly defiance that struck me, it was his voice. He sounded like Daddy. I ran beneath the frame to hear him better, but Miss Olsen picked me up and put me to one side.

"Virgil," she said, "you know what happened when you were sassy to me last year. Do you want me to have another talk with your father?"

He shook his head like the Angus bull and slid down the pole, hulking off toward the trees near the boys' outhouse. I followed him.

"Virgil—"

"Get away from me, you little shit!"

Delighted with the vocal timbre I had missed with an almost physical pain, I didn't care what Virgil said as long as he went on talking. I'd never heard the word *shit* in my entire life and wasn't concerned with its meaning.

"Talk, Virgil."

"You shut up and leave me alone, or I'll take you in there and ram you down headfirst."

"I didn't know you *could* talk," I said, greedy for any sound he might make.

He wheeled with a roar and knocked me down, jarring me so hard that I saw colored spots before my eyes. I held my breath, fighting the fierce urge to hurt him back. Virgil was not a chair that bumped my shin or a cat that scratched my arm. Getting back at Virgil would start an unending cycle of pain. Besides, I didn't want to make him even madder. I needed to be near him to hear him speak.

For several days I dogged his steps, delighting in his spoken abuse, but the arm-twisting was too much. I made the mistake of telling Mom. When she came to school with me and sat there all day, Virgil left me alone and didn't say a word. It was terrible.

Even when I was on my own again, Virgil acted as if I weren't there—until I made it impossible for him to ignore me. I was scared to put dirt in his lunch bucket, but I did it, and I made sure that he saw me do it. Unfortunately his reaction was silent and physical. His big hands twisted the skin of my wrist until it burned like fire and nearly tore. Having pondered boundaries—where the thing that was "I" met the rest of creation—I knew that I must not let Virgil touch me again. It was too humiliating. However, I still meant to have what I needed from him—the sound of his voice.

On the way to school the next morning, I went down the Larsons' lane, ducked behind the blue blaze of morning-glories, and found a hiding place in the bushes. After what seemed like a long time, Virgil and two other boys came along. They were talking. I ignored the words and soaked up the sound of his voice, wanting it to go on forever, but it was fading with distance. How could I hang onto it?

"Virgil Denkman is a big dummy!" I yelled.

"Where are you, you little shithead?"

"Boy, is she ever stuck on you, Virg."

I couldn't see whether they were coming back, because I was down on my stomach to keep my light dress from showing through the bushes. I chewed my knuckles because my nails were too nasty to nibble. Mom had put saffron on my fingers to break me of nail-biting, and the awful taste simply wouldn't wash off.

"I'll catch her at recess and pound her," Virgil said. "Can't do it now 'cause there's Old Lady Olsen with her goldarned bell."

That meant I'd have to run into the open immediately or be late, and if Virgil saw me, he wouldn't wait until recess to pound me. I decided I'd rather be late. However, I had still another option. Why go to school at all? I could stay with Shirley Larson all day and yell at Virgil again when he went home.

Shirley was stirring something in a bowl when I peered through the screen door. When she felt my eyes on her, she looked up.

"Why, Margaret, you sure did give me a turn," she said. "I *thought* somebody was at the door, but I was looking too high. Isn't it time you were in school?"

"Miss Olsen sent me home." The lie came easily because that sort of thing did happen. Miss Olsen had sent Maxine Werley home because she wet her pants, but I certainly wasn't going to offer that reason. I added, "She said I needed quiet." That was what Aunt Kam had to have when she choked.

Shirley motioned for me to come in. When I had shooed the flies and edged through the door, she felt my forehead with a hand warmed by wielding the big wooden spoon.

"You don't look sick to me, but if Miss Olsen wants you to go home, I guess I can run you over when Klaus gets back with the car."

"Oh, I can't go home. Mom's in the field and Grandma's sick."

"Mrs. Jorgen's sick? How come I didn't hear about it? I listened in on all the rings yesterday and today."

"Oh, we don't talk about it. It's just a thing she has."

"My, my. Well, in that case, I guess you'd better stay here and keep me company. When you have nothing but boys, you spend a lot of time alone in the kitchen. It's nice to have a little girl to talk to when you're baking."

It was a good morning. I scraped batter and frosting bowls, played the piano in the parlor, and picked some early asters. When Klaus came from the field for his noon meal, he asked what I was doing there, and Shirley repeated my invention.

"Hadn't you better call Petra?"

"Let her have some peace, poor woman. I'll talk to her when I take Margaret home."

It was good to sit at the table with Klaus, breathing in his mannish smell and watching his big hands cut and spear the food. I even liked the dirt-filled wrinkles that criss-crossed the back of his neck.

"How you gettin' along in school, Margaret?" he asked.

"Fair-to-middlin'," I said, aping Cliff Potter's tone when he didn't like something but didn't want to say so. "Can I go to the barn with you?"

"Nope, I've got no call to go to the barn until milking time, and you won't be here then."

"Klaus, it wouldn't kill you to show her around a little while your food is digesting."

"She's seen barns before, and there's nothing special about ours, but—if you say so. We'll go after I get the market report."

I told Klaus that he didn't have to take me. I'd changed my mind. If Shirley had to make him do it, we wouldn't have any fun. I'd already figured out that sometimes you lost when you won.

All afternoon I watched the angle of the sun carefully, trying to match the remembered slant of light at the hour when school was let out. I couldn't read clocks, and I didn't want to ask Shirley the time.

"You're antsy as a pup on hot tar," she said. "Want me to drive you home now?"

"Oh, no, pretty soon I'll start walking."

"But I was going to talk to your mother—"

"She's too busy to talk today."

When the light looked right, I said good-bye. Shirley watched from the door, forcing me to walk up the lane to the road. As soon as she turned away, I doubled back and hid in the bushes. The little kids came past and after what seemed like hours, Virgil came. Alone and mute, he zig-zagged to kick clods on both sides of the road.

"Virgil!" I called in a high falsetto.

"Who's there?"

Afraid to speak because he was so close, I cackled like a hen.

"No goddam chicken can say my name," he muttered to himself, "and it ain't the Langelund kid because she's home sick." He shrugged and walked on.

When he was out of sight, I cut across the fields to go home. Keeping to the road past the Denkman farm was too dangerous. The short-cut also allowed me to dump the contents of my lunch-box in the backhouse, circle back to the lane, and make a normal entrance to greet my extremely healthy grandmother. I had told Shirley some of the truth, at least. Mom really was in the field.

The next morning I repeated the taunting of Virgil from behind the bushes and reappeared in the Larsons' kitchen. Shirley was testing the heat of a flatiron with a dampened finger. It hissed satisfactorily.

"What, again?"

"Miss Olsen talked to Mom. I'm supposed to ask if I can stay here today, too."

"Of course you can, but I can't imagine why Petra doesn't ring me up about it."

"The line's always busy."

"Well, I guess! Ruby Denkman has been talking to her cousin Emma since breakfast. She had the nerve to say, 'Isn't that right, Shirley?' I didn't say a word—just pressed the hook down real slow."

We had some nice times, Shirley and I, for almost two weeks. Then Miss Olsen's car turned down our lane, and it was all over. I wasn't spanked, but there are worse punishments. If I had gone to school instead of staying with Shirley all those days, maybe we would have stayed on the farm, and I could have been a 4-H girl. Mom got so upset about what I did that she got an auctioneer to sell all the animals—even Sofus—and the tractor and the manure spreader. We went to live in Grandma's dark blue house in Harlan without any animals, and I never heard Virgil say another word.

Love

from *Amalie's Story*

[7]

ONE EARLY SEPTEMBER MORNING not long after I came home from Sandinge I offered to hang up the sheets behind the trees of the lower garden. This was Hop-Caroline's job, but I had noticed that she was getting older, and the heavy weight of a basket of wet linens nearly overbalanced her. It was to be a warm, green and gold day, but the grass gleamed with dew, and I walked barefoot to the lines with my steaming, lye-scented load. As I approached, two black and white magpies took to the air noisily. Their clamor alerted the white doves that gave our home its name, bringing them from their cotes in a burst like an out-of-season snowstorm. I stood still for a moment to watch them descend on the grain Sven Rasmussen had scattered for them, then tucked up my skirt, knotted a kerchief over my hair, and rolled my sleeves.

As I flung the hot, wet sheets over the line, I heard wheels rolling along the road from Ausig, but I didn't look around until a man's voice called out, *"God dag!* Can you tell me the whereabouts of Herr Shipowner Ormstrup?"

I whirled, snatching the kerchief from my hair and pulling the hem of my skirt from my waistband. I supposed the stranger had appraised a completely immodest stretch of bare leg at some length before he spoke.

He was the best-looking man I ever had seen as he sat there in a shiny, red-trimmed trap behind a glossy black horse. His chestnut hair and goatee glinted in the sun, which threw a shadow of his strong nose and chin on the sheet I had just smoothed. His full lips stretched in a smile.

"Don't be bashful, charming as it is. I need information, my girl!"

Your girl indeed, I thought. *What do you take me for?*

He cocked his head to consider me. "You were such a picture before I surprised you! The best of the land, noble in the simplicity of your dignified labor—but now you've become self-conscious.

Too bad!"

I knew then what I had to deal with. Here was a peasant worshiper of the deepest dye. Normally I would have laughed at such pretensions, but those hazel eyes almost the color of dark amber held too many complications for quick dismissal. I remembered Jette's words, "We must seem to be what men imagine. They invent the women they love." This man who still waited for me to speak had invented a peasant girl, and that was what I would be, for there was a sudden heat between us. I felt it, and he must have, for the reins slipped from his hands as we stared at each other.

I finally found my voice and told him, "Herr Shipowner Ormstrup is taking his coffee in the garden."

"I will ask your master if I may take you for a drive when my business with him is finished."

"No!" I said. "He would not allow it. When you have finished your business, I will meet you at the edge of the heath—just over there." I pointed to a spot not visible from the windows of Dovedale and turned back to my work as he drove on.

When I had stretched the remaining sheets haphazardly on the line, I hurried to the spot. I pinched my cheeks furiously, then decided it was too soon. The color would fade before he came. I pulled off some purple broom to thrust into my hair, but the steam had straightened the curls left over from the Sabbath, and the flowers slipped out as quickly as I put them in.

Why didn't he hurry? But if he did, what would I say? I didn't know his name, and he didn't know mine. The whole thing was insane! I got up from the heather to run away, only to come back and throw myself down to wait.

When he did come, he left the trap in the road and walked to me. He had a handsome stride that bit off distance as if he owned the heath. His pockets were full of Mor's almond cookies, and he was delighted with himself for managing an unexpected treat for me.

Assuming there was nothing about me to be told, that I was the personification of all the general peasant virtues—and vices, I suppose—he told me about himself. He was Peter Jorgen from the island of Funen, where his parents lived in a manor house his twin brothers would inherit. The law of primogeniture being no respecter of station, he had gone to business rather than to the Church, and he had come to Ausig to discuss an important arrangement with

Herr Shipowner Ormstrup.

"He is a good businessman," he said. "I think we will have a long and fruitful association—unless he finds out that I mean to steal you! One cannot find good workers as in the old days."

"Have you tried the Girl Market?"

"Let *him* go there, for I will have you!" He leaned close to me. "And not for work!"

"But I know how to do everything!"

"I'm sure you do," he said, and kissed me until I was as weak as when I fell in the snow on my way to Holger Danske. I struggled, knowing I could not claim his kiss until he knew who I was.

"I will be missed if I don't go back!"

"We can meet tonight. I have been invited to return for *middag.*"

"Things may be different tonight," I warned.

He bowed, as he had been taught, no doubt in the manor house on Funen. "I must have something of yours to touch until we meet again."

I pulled the amber cross from my neck and dropped it into his palm, leaving him to puzzle over its fine quality.

That night I was late coming to the table, and Mor sent Hop-Caroline upstairs for me. I had been crying and sighing all afternoon, afraid to face Peter Jorgen after my deception. I had, however, put on my newest dress of deep blue silk and was ready except for my hair, which Hop-Caroline unceremoniously raked with a brush. At the door I broke from her clutch and unstoppered Jette's perfume to scent the base of my throat.

"So you've heard what a fine young cock we have at table tonight!" she chortled.

I moaned.

Peter Jorgen rose when I entered the room, completely concealing the confusion he must have felt. He followed Mor's conversational lead for a while, then branched out on his own topics, chiefly the refusal of the University of Copenhagen to install Georg Brandes in the Chair of Belles Lettres because he had said that Jesus Christ would diminish in importance as Thor and Odin had.

"A terrible thing!" Mor said.

"Indeed it is!" Peter said. "No professor should be measured by his orthodoxy."

Mor tightened her lips, for she had meant that Brandes' views were terrible, and Peter quickly changed the subject to performances he had lately seen at the Royal Theatre: a Holberg comedy and the dancing of *Coppelia.*

When Far suggested that I show the garden to our guest, Peter pulled back my chair with great courtliness and draped my shawl around my shoulders.

As we walked in the cool night without a word, I lost the poise of the dinner table completely. I was terrified of the coming showdown. All at once Peter started to laugh. It was a great, booming, unfettered sound—the laughter of Funen, whose people are called the Bavarians of Denmark.

Relieved and angry at the same time, I said, "I'm glad that we have afforded you some amusement during your visit."

"Frøken Nielsen, you are all women rolled into one! What an exquisite joke!"

"Then you aren't angry?"

"Angry? I'm delighted! I can't afford a mistress, and my parents are scarcely emancipated enough to accept a peasant daughter-in-law, so your true identity solves my problem. Will you have me?"

"But we are strangers to each other!"

"Stop making foolish objections. We both know what we know, is that not true? We have known since this morning."

"Say my name."

"Amalie!" He made it sound rich and queenly, as I thought it should, and I went to him gladly.

This was my own fairy tale, I thought, until he released me and gave me a slap on the rear that stung right through my petticoats. Throwing his head back with that lusty Funen laugh, he said, "Our children will outnumber the bastards of Christian IV!"

[8]

Peter and I were to be married on June 5, Danish Constitution Day. He argued that it should be much sooner, but I had been reading when I might have been sewing on the obligatory dozen of everything that a bride must bring to her marriage, and besides, Far wanted us to know each other better.

Gradual discovery was impossible for us because Peter traveled in his business, but when he came to Dovedale, our betrothal allowed us to be alone together, and we took full advantage of the privilege up to a point. I was unwilling to go the way of Hanne Eskildsen, who had borne a husky baby boy six months after her wedding day.

Between Peter's widely spaced visits, I embroidered linens until my eyes watered, hoping to finish everything but the monograms, which could not be stitched until after the ceremony. I sewed secretly in my room on the Sabbath, risking the penalty of taking those stitches up with my nose in heaven. Heaven could wait, but Peter couldn't!

We were apart at Christmas, when every Dane goes home if he has to crawl. Thinking of Peter on Funen, I stood apart from the celebration of Dovedale, wasting what would be my last Yule at Ausig.

A candle shone from every window and a sheaf of rye for the birds was nailed to the hitching post in the courtyard. Hop-Caroline, now completely gray, hobbled to the attic with a dish of porridge for *nissen,* the Christmas elf, and the red-berried Christ's-thorn crowned every doorway.

Dovedale was filled with neighbors and friends all the twelve days of Christmas. If anyone should go out of the house without partaking of its cheer, they would bear our Yule away, and though no one refused our sweets and ale, Mor took the extra precaution of filling the pockets of departing guests with peppernuts.

On Christmas Eve, the lucky almond in the pudding fell to me. I think Hop-Caroline nudged the treasure my way, but all to no avail, for luck cannot be manipulated.

In early January, I developed a fever that baffled the doctor in Ausig. Tossing in delirium, I asked for what I dared not request when I was in full possession of myself; the presence of my real mother and my brother Ib at the wedding. Far promised to send for them, thinking I would not live to hold him to his word. I had no intention of dying, and my greatest suffering was the dread of having Peter see me as I was. My hair came out in great clumps, and Hop-Caroline told me I looked like a starved horse.

"Some bride you will be!" she said with cheerful malice on a dark day in February when I was inspecting myself in a hand mirror. Luckily for her, I was too weak to throw the glass.

I ordered all mirrors to be taken from my room and set about willing myself to be well. By mid-May, my hair had grown back in a soft aureole, but the emaciation was stubborn, and the fitting of my wedding gown could wait no longer. The seamstress from Ausig moved into an upstairs room to fly at the task of cutting down the ivory silk wedding dress and the seven trousseau costumes made when I was in full health.

Heartsick over my skeletal appearance, I resorted to Jette's suggestion of handkerchiefs in the bodice, then worried about cheating Peter.

He came to Dovedale two days before the wedding, and when I saw the familiar trap enter the courtyard, I turned from the window and cried. Then, hearing his voice booming in the rooms below, I lost my pride in the longing to see him.

Nothing fit me but my trousseau dresses. I put on the pale blue linen and started down the stairs clutching the railing. The upturned faces of Far, Mor, and Hop-Caroline blurred, and I saw only the hugeness of Peter as he took the stairs in a few strides to lift me and carry me down.

"Amalie, my dearest love! What has happened to you? Why wasn't I told?"

"I wouldn't allow it. I had hoped to be better by now, but the fever has made me ugly, and if you don't want me like this, you are free!"

Mor touched Far's arm and they started toward the parlor, sweeping Hop-Caroline with them to leave us alone.

"Nothing could make me stop wanting you! I have a strange fever too, Amalie, I burn for your very bones!"

"They are very close to the surface, as you see."

"I see with my heart," he said, and kissed me very gently. I had not known he could be gentle. "Funen will make you well!"

If he could love me as I was now, what could ever part us? I asked him to carry me to the parlor, where I sat up straight on the lion head sofa and asked Far when my real mother would arrive.

"She is taking the train to Tylstrup, and Sven will meet her there tomorrow. I wonder how we will find each other after so many years?" He sighed heavily.

I saw then that Far had aged without my notice. Absorbed in my own affairs, I had failed to see the deep lines around his eyes and the sag of his once-firm cheeks. I realized too that my mother would not look as I had imagined her all my life. Far's image of her as a blooming, young woman was also mine, and I wondered if I could bear to alter it. Still, I wanted old questions answered before I started a new life with Peter.

My love was beside me, wordlessly calming my agitation with the pressure of his arm, when Sven drove into the courtyard with my mother.

Bodil Ormstrup Nielsen Pedersen was alone in the back of the carriage. She sat straight-backed with one gloved hand resting on a small suitcase. Work-worn, tired, but still proud, she was dressed all in gray, and conscious of the newness of her clothing. She barely touched the supporting hand Sven offered as she gathered her skirts to step down.

Staring at her, I saw an older version of myself. We had the same strong nose, full lips, and wide-set eyes. Her body was slightly fuller than mine had been before the fever.

"Amalie?"

With a slight pressure of his hand, Peter stepped back, and when I turned to present him, he was at the other side of the courtyard beckoning to Sven.

"*Are* you Amalie?" she asked, and I could only nod. I didn't know what to call her. Not "Mor," and certainly not "Fru Pedersen." Nor could I call her "Bodil."

She took my hands and looked into my eyes. All strangeness melted in our tears as we embraced. For all the care Mor had given me, I never had had this fierce, unquestioning caring from her.

I saw Far's face in the window and knew that he was fighting the tears that only women were allowed. Then he was running into the courtyard to hug his sister so roughly that her bonnet fell off. Mor came from the doorway to welcome her sister-in-law to Dovedale, and with the three of us talking at once, we made slow progress to the house.

"Where is my brother Ib?"

"Gone to *Amerika.* He is a Mormon now—"

"And Tinus Pedersen?" Far asked.

"Dead these six months. Tuberculosis, they said. Now Karsten, what have you done to this girl? I gave you a fat, rosy baby, and look at her now! Ah, Maren, how long it has been—"

I turned from the happy tangle of reunion to see Peter watching us with his hands in his pockets—an outsider. I would not have it so. As I presented him to my mother, my legs weakened under me, and he took me to the garden to rest on the bench under the shade of the beeches.

"A new mother and a new husband at the same time is too much for anyone," he said.

"What do you think of my mother?"

"She is a good woman."

"Is that all you can say about her?"

"What you cannot say briefly, you do not know."

Because of my physical weakness, tears came with little provocation, and I found slights where none were intended. If Peter found my mother so unremarkable, how would be look upon me as I aged? As I pulled away from him in my unreasonable hurt, a shocking oversight of my own occurred to me.

"Peter! What about *your* parents? When are they coming?"

"They are here—at the inn in Ausig. When I told my mother of your illness, she refused to lay the burden of meeting upon you before the wedding. She says you can come to know each other at Fairwoods."

"But I would think she would want to look me over—decide whether I will do as a wife for you!"

Peter laughed. "She knows that the matter is beyond her say!" Then he kissed me with a controlled intensity that charged the very air around us.

I went to bed in the middle of the afternoon to store up strength for the next day, but I didn't sleep. Peter came and went in the room, Far and Mor were in and out with a hovering concern, and Hop-Caroline sat at the foot of my bed to chatter about the preparations whenever she could escape her part in them.

"They have put up the two masts with the welcome banner and the garland of fir is on the door—the flags must wait until tomorrow, in case it rains in the night—Herr Ormstrup has gone to the attic for the painted shields—oh, it will be so fine!" She clapped her hands like a young girl.

Seeing the fold of a gray skirt at the edge of the door, I called, "Please come in!"

My real mother entered the room with quiet diffidence and sat in the chair Hop-Caroline pulled close to the bed.

"Two mothers you have," Hop-Caroline observed as she hobbled away. "You will have all the advice that any bride could wish!"

"What advice do I need?" I asked when we were alone.

"Much cannot be told," she said in a slow, measured way that showed she had given the matter considerable thought. "Your Peter can provide for you?"

"Oh yes, he is very clever in business."

"That's good, for when the stall is empty, the horses bite each other."

"Has the stall been empty for you?"

"Sometimes, Amalie, not always. Karsten has helped many times. Your husband will be away from you much of the time?"

"I suppose so. He travels as far as Hamburg and Paris."

She sighed. "It has always been for women to wait. They might as well learn it first as last. Well, you do love him, I can see that. I saw you with him in the garden, and there was a glow around the two of you like the ring around the moon when the weather is about to change. It was like that with me and Niels Ibsen."

Since she had opened the door to the question that troubled me most, I seized the chance to ask it.

"I—I have been sick. How much strength does it take to—to be a wife to a man?"

She laughed. "If your Peter had been the one with the fever, you might worry, for they say, 'When the Devil is ill, a monk he would be, but when he is well, then a devil is he!' But a woman can give herself no matter how she feels—can if she will. At first, take your pleasure in his, and when you are well, your own joy will catch up with you!"

I caught her hand and kissed the work-roughened palm, feeling closer to her than I ever had to Mor. "Oh, why didn't you keep me?"

She averted her face. "As Karsten has told you, I hope, I loved you and wanted you to have a better life."

"But which would have been better?" I cried.

"What's done is done."

In the morning, I felt uncommonly well. I hummed to myself as Mor, my mother, and Hop-Caroline helped me dress and assured me that the many tucks in the ivory silk concealed my wasted condition.

The guests would arrive for *snaps* and ale at ten, and I would sit behind closed doors in the parlor, unseen until I was seated in the carriage for the ride to the church. Hurrying through the rose-filled rooms, I reached my hiding place as the first carriage stopped in the courtyard.

My future in-laws alighted from the rented barouche. Herr Jorgen was a portly man who walked with a cane, and I diagnosed a case of gout from his heavily veined red nose. Clearly he was an active man who bore his hindering affliction with impatience. As he stood in the sunny courtyard taking in Dovedale with a sweeping glance, I saw much of Peter in him.

Fru Jorgen was tall and slender in a watered-silk gown the color of a thrush's wing. She had a porcelain refinement of feature seldom seen in our region of North Jutland, and the hand she placed on Sven's arm as she stepped down was as white as the meat of an almond. She was a queen, I thought, staring at her in awed admiration. She seemed to float between the greenery-twined masts that held the welcome banner, and I felt a twinge of black jealousy. Her presence would take all eyes from the bride.

But later, when the guests crowded around the flower-decked carriage to admire me, she stood back, smiling at me from a distance as she let me have my day. When the laughing, jostling neighbors hurried to their own carriages to begin the ride to the church, she moved close enough to say, "Lucky the bride the sun shines on!"

At the church, Peter lifted me down, and Pastor Madsen walked through the open doors to meet us and lead us inside, where candles flickered in the swimming green light.

The strength I had felt earlier was ebbing away, and the bridal wreath of myrtle weighed heavily on my head. I drew on the vitality of Peter standing so straight beside me, raising my chin to lock it in an imaginary vise. I'm sure that Pastor Madsen shortened his sermon to save my meager strength, for I remember little more than the solemn vows we took.

Then we were in the sun again, smiling from the flowery carriage at the head of the procession. Whips cracked and guns went off; horses reared and women screamed. The noise was joyful, but it made me tremble, and Peter put a protective arm around me.

At Dovedale, a band of musicians from Brønderslev struck up a new tune every time a carriage set down a load of wedding guests. House and garden were aswarm with visitors eating, drinking, and talking gaily.

Peter took me straight to my room and put me to bed, insisting that I sleep while he sat beside me holding my hand.

"Lock the door," I said, and when he had, I threw back the cover and held out my arms to him. What a picture I must have made with those thin arms poking out of a welter of bridal petticoats!

He began a solicitous protest, then broke off with a burst of laughter and came to me. In that narrow, girlish bed with a myrtle blossom wreath hanging rakishly on its headpost, we both forgot that I was a near invalid. Warned by my mother not to expect pleasure at first, I gave myself to the encounter with a fierce interest. So this was what a man was like! The hardness, the hairiness, the power, all of it mine! I took it greedily, even the pain, as we met each other and fell back like the waters of Skagen.

Later, when we came downstairs for the food, speeches, and dancing, Far remarked on my improved color and said the rest must have done me good. I smiled and walked with my arm in Peter's to the center table, where a flowerbed of blossoms surrounded a huge, flat cake decorated with our initials in raspberry jam. Understanding the jokes and glances of our friends better than they knew, I cut the first piece of cake and stood back to gaze at the tall candles burning at each end of the table. They represented Peter and me, and if both flamed until midnight, we would have a long life together. The wax was of the best quality, and the wicks were strong.

Just before midnight, I saw that one of the candles was missing from its holder. It worried me, but when I mentioned it to Peter, he said, "Never mind, some prankish boy has run away with it. Come, the carriage is ready!"

Driving under an arch of flowers and then between a double row of torches along the lane, I looked back at my family in the lighted door of Dovedale. I couldn't see their faces, but their arms were uplifted in farewell, and I could hear them shouting, "God bless!"

from *Petra*

[19]

IN THE NINTH YEAR OF our marriage, we sold the farm on Wisconsin Ridge and bought another in the rich bottomland of the East Nishnabotna. It bordered Soren's former land, which made it seem like home.

"This is where we'll stay, Petra. The land rises and falls like my father's—my blood seems to remember it."

The house was pleasant, with doors and porches to the north and west and a back stoop reaching into a sunny south yard. The kitchen caught the sunrise and sunset. Even on a cloudy day it was filled with clear, gray light. A pass-through to the dining room was cut in the north wall. A small eastern alcove off the dining room held my sewing machine, the new radio, and Lauritz's easy chair. Between our bedroom in the southwest corner and the parlor in the northwest was a stairway to the second floor; here the roof sloped down on two bedrooms and a wide hall that would hold a bed if need be.

In the parlor was the old treadle organ from the Merrill's Grove Baptist church. Though I couldn't play, Lauritz had bought it for me when the church got a new one, and I enjoyed pumping asthmatic triads from it whenever I had a spare moment.

The Merrill's Grove church provided all the social life we required: pot-luck suppers and Ladies' Aid meetings.

We were less than a mile from the village of Fiscus, and I would walk down the hill to shop at the general store, admiring the bright orange gasoline in the pumps outside and listening to the heavy hum of the grinders at the grain elevator. I never had much to carry home because we grew most of our own food. I cooked with butter and cream and gave the leftovers to Sofus, the half-breed collie Lauritz had brought home from a farm sale.

Lauritz was digging a single ditch through the valley of the south field to replace the triplet streams from the Nishnabotna that made a broadening fan of land untillable, and I was busy with quilting. All in all, we had reached a harbor of contentment, with one day following the next in easy rhythm. In God and Herbert Hoover we trusted, shutting our ears to the distant echoes of gangster gunfire and flapper shrieks.

Stig brought his bride home at corn-picking time, and Betty spent long days alone in the house while the rest of us strapped our wrists with husking hooks and went into the fields with mules and wagon. Working a row next to my brother's I tried to outdo him, but two of his ears hit the sideboards for every one of mine. I blamed it on the fact that I wasn't feeling up to par. I could scarcely bear to scramble the breakfast eggs, and Betty's early morning cigarette made me queasy. If I wasn't better soon, I meant to see a doctor.

"Hey Lauritz," Stig said, "why don't you buy a tractor? How you can stand these cussed mules is more than I know!"

"I've been thinking of it."

I fired a runt ear at Fritz's rump and missed, jubilant at the thought that his days were numbered.

Having spurned breakfast, I was hungry, but when we went to the house at noon, I recoiled from the canned spaghetti Betty had ladled onto plates.

"Wish I could do better by you," she said, "but I just can't get the hang of cooking." She lit a cigarette and played with the belt of her kimono.

"It's not that, Betty—"

"Old Betty's got other specialties," Stig said, grabbing at her. "She's my little old ripe peach!"

"Stig, you shouldn't! Not in front of your sister!"

"She knows the worst."

I tried to smile at Betty, wondering if Stig could be happy with this plumpish brown-haired girl for life. I was disappointed in his choice, for I had envisioned a young version of Lily Hertert as his mate—a strong, beautiful, intelligent woman whose superiority would no doubt make me jealous.

Stig and Betty went to town every night and drank. When they drove their car into the south yard and knocked over the pump, the damage chastened them, and sobriety attended the rest of their visit.

While they were waiting in the yard to say good-bye, I was vomiting in the outhouse. As I came toward them, shaky and teary-eyed, Stig winked at me and said, "I'll have Old Betty in the same shape before you can say 'Jack Robinson'! Happy hatching!"

Lauritz and I looked at each other, stunned.

Stig laughed uproariously. "Just look at 'em! Abraham and Sarah!"

"Who are they?" Betty asked.

"Bible types. Don't you know anything?"

Betty's lip quivered. "You don't need to make fun of me."

No one must quarrel in the morning of my miracle. I dashed to a sheltered border of chrysanthemums that had escaped the frost, tearing up yellow and russet blooms to thrust into Stig's hands.

"Give these to your wife and tell her you're sorry."

He did, and they drove away with Betty melting into his shoulder. We watched them to the end of the lane.

Lauritz closed his eyes, moving his lips. Then he kissed me and said, "Let's go to town and find the doctor."

Doctor Gus's office was close to the farm implement showroom, but Lauritz didn't even glance at the window as we passed.

"Aren't you even going to look?"

"The tractor will have to wait. Just now, everything must be for the baby."

"But what if—what if it isn't true?"

"It is. I know it!"

Doctor Gus rumpled his thinning tangle of gray curls. "Where else but in the medical profession can you say the same thing to two women in the same day and get reactions of suicidal gloom and Christmas morning!"

"Which woman am I?" I asked fearfully.

"The other was an unmarried sixteen-year-old."

I rushed from the office to the waiting room, shouting, "Lauritz, it's true!" We would have caught hands and danced in the ring of waiting patients if Doctor Gus hadn't bellowed after me, "Petra! I'm not through with you."

I returned to him meekly and listened to him say, "You're pretty old for a first baby, but it's been done. We'll get you through."

"I don't care if I die," I said rapturously. "Just let me see the baby first!"

"You'll see more of that baby than you care to," he snorted. "Jorgen women don't die that way."

Mama told me the same thing as I crushed her fingers through the most massive pain I had ever endured. It was Midsummer's Eve and the southwest bedroom was hot and still, heavy with the smell of disinfectant. Doctor Gus, inhuman in a gauze mask, pressed hard on my stomach until I shrieked.

"Hard pelvic bones, but thank God she's wide," he muttered, thrusting a shiny instrument between my sheet-tented knees.

"What's that?" I whimpered.

"Shoe horn."

I cried for Lauritz, but Mama wouldn't let him in. "This is not for a man to see," she said, and I had to be content with the sound of his voice through the door.

"I'm here! I love you!"

I thought the ceiling was lowering as the face cone hovered sweetishly, and then I was falling away from the pain.

When I opened my eyes, I could not recognize the flat body under the sheet as my own. I had died, I was convinced, and I felt a languid curiosity about my new state. The faces looming in the gauzy light of kerosene lamps were familiar—Lauritz and Mama. Mama placed something between my flat nonbody and my limp arm.

"A girl," she said, "and girls born on Midsummer's Eve will be beautiful and drive men mad."

"Let's name her Margaret—for the great uncrowned queen of Denmark," Lauritz said.

I nodded, straining to look at the small Margaret. Beautiful? Her head had corners (forceps, Dr. Gus had told Mama), yet she was beautiful to me. What she would do to men was too far in the future to worry about. I sighed and folded her close, awed by the rich variousness of love as my free hand stretched to my husband and my mother.

"Thanks be to God!" Lauritz said.

Yes, thanks be to Him. In the curious beauty of mixed joy and pain, I had forgotten to say it, but my whole being said it for me. We had everything we could possibly want, and surely this June of 1929 was the beginning of the millennium for us.

Margaret used the deep basket that had been my infant bed until Lauritz finished the crib he was making from banana crates. Not that she was in it much, for I carried her about while I did everything that could be accomplished with one hand.

Though it was high summer, I wrapped her in flannel to shield her from any possible breeze, and she developed an angry outbreak of prickly heat.

She screamed with colic most of her waking hours, and when she was asleep I was terrified, either by her light breathing or by her snorts and snuffles.

My anxiety for Margaret's survival dried up the milk in my breasts, but once she was on a boiled formula, she began to thrive.

"I feel terrible that I can't feed her," I told Lauritz. "Mama nursed eight babies!"

"Maybe it's better like this. *I* can hold a bottle too."

He could and did. We came very close to fighting for the privilege, and I took a selfish pleasure in the feedings that occurred while he was in the fields.

I had stayed out of sight during the months of obvious pregnancy, even going so far as to listen to radio sermons instead of going to church with Lauritz, and now the neighbors thought we had adopted a child. I didn't know about the talk going around until our neighbors, Cliff and Anna Potter, came to see Margaret.

"You sure picked out a good one," Cliff said.

"I always wondered how that worked," Anna went on. "Do they let you go right in and choose the one you want?"

"What are you talking about?"

Anna was abashed. "I guess we're out of line to ask questions like that, but we've never known anybody who adopted a baby."

I laughed incredulously. "She's ours! Can't you see that she looks just like Lauritz?"

Cliff leaned over the basket. "Hmm. Well, I will say they broke the mold when they made that one!"

I thought so too, and I dreamed of a vague future greatness for Margaret. Kamille had cut a picture of Queen Marie of Romania from the paper, prophesying that Margaret would grow up to resemble her. I tucked it into the Bible for future reference.

Margaret was certain to outshine her cousins, even Geraldine, who had just been voted the University of Nebraska's Million Dollar Girl because she looked a lot like Jean Harlow.

Margaret sat up for the first time the day after the market crash, and she started to talk in the week the banks closed in Harlan. The gravity of these events barely distracted us from our preoccupation with Margaret. Our land was paid for and safe. We three could live in a world apart.

Or could we? When John Hertert shot himself, I realized the desperate seriousness of what was happening. John had been a banker for half a century. He stood for all that was solid and secure.

"He felt that the worst was yet to come," Lily Hertert said, "and he couldn't bear it. The day he pulled the curtains down, he saw the faces of the small depositors pressing against the glass. People he'd helped through the years with loans at low interest were cursing him, and it broke his heart!"

"Whose fault *is* it?" I asked.

"The industrial plant of the country is overbuilt," she explained dully, "and we can't consume what we make."

"Then we should stop making things."

"We will," she said, "we will, and everything will stand still."

"The land will go on growing things."

"Yes, and no one will have money to buy them."

I shrugged. "That's nothing new. We haven't gotten a decent price for stock or grain in years, but we have plenty for ourselves."

We did eat well. The rub came when we wanted to buy something.

"The ditch in the south pasture is too wide and deep to drive across now," Lauritz said. "I'll have to build a bridge."

"We can stop at the lumberyard after we've been to Mama's."

"No, I'm afraid we can't, and we won't be able to come to town as often. We can't spare money for gas."

As we entered the blue house, it occurred to me that I hadn't thought to worry about Mama's finances. Now I was almost afraid to ask, but I did.

"Mama, did you lose much when the bank closed?"

"About half. Much as I trusted John Hertert, I always kept a strongbox by me, and I'll bet your husband has done the same."

"Did you, Lauritz?"

He nodded sheepishly. "I didn't want you to know, because it's like burying your talents in the ground—they don't grow—but I'm enough of a Dane to play it safe."

"Hope for the best and prepare for the worst," Mama said. "I'm surprised that Karl Tilberg didn't do as much. He's in real trouble!"

Karl's hardware stock was frozen on the shelves, which, he said gloomily, was just as well, because he couldn't have replaced anything he sold. He let his clerks go and spent long, lonely days in the store.

Somehow Karl and Kamille found the gas to visit us on the farm every weekend. I knew the meals I cooked for them were the only substantial ones they had, because of the revealing remarks of Else's children.

After we finished a Sunday dinner of roast beef, Jack Russell eyed the remains. "We could eat for a week on that!"

"Jack!" Kamille protested.

"It's true! You've been using the same old worn-out soup bone since last Sunday!"

"Kamille," I said, "are things that bad?"

Marianne volunteered, "We have to stay in the kitchen all the time because the rest of the house is cold."

Kamille covered her face and wept. Karl looked at his plate and spoke in a dead voice. "I've been borrowing against my life insurance, but it lapses next month."

I looked at Lauritz, and we both spoke at once. "Would you like to come to us until things are better?"

Karl laughed bitterly. "We might be here the rest of our lives! No thank you, we'll manage. Come on, Lauritz, I'll earn my dinner by helping you tear down that shed."

They worked until dusk, pulling out nails and stacking the boards that would become a bridge across the south pasture gully. Lauritz had felled trees for the supports.

I sent Jack Russell and Marianne to gather eggs to have a chance to talk to Kamille privately.

"Wouldn't you like to leave the children here? It wouldn't hurt them to go to country school for a while."

"No, Petra, I can't do without them."

Now that we had Margaret, I really didn't want more children around. To offer and be refused was the perfect solution for me, yet I was amazed at my sister. Like Valborg, she put her own feelings first. The best thing for the children was secondary. Lauritz and I lived for Margaret, probably because she came to us after such long yearning.

Looking through the window at Margaret's white-blonde head bent over a hole she was digging with an old tablespoon, I melted with love. Sofus ran up to her and knocked her over with an excess of doggy affection, but she was up immediately, laughing at his efforts to enlarge her excavation with his paws.

Margaret and Sofus bathed in golden light, Lauritz silhouetted at his work, and the warmth of that setting sun on my face shaped a rare moment of content.

from *The Sailing Out*

[20]

I WASN'T THE ONLY ONE who changed during that time in Rochester. When I came back, I discovered that Wyonne Shenk's waist was smaller and her bra size was a proud 36C. Wyonne approved of the fleshier me, which caused me to spend more time with her than I did with Lotus and Monica. Mom didn't approve.

"Why don't you like Wyonne?" I asked. "You used to."

"She's fast, that's why."

My understanding of that term was vague, and it seemed best to skirt it, so I simply said, "She's fun, though."

"So I gather."

Mom let it go at that and didn't discuss Wyonne again until the question of the double date came up. Wyonne knew a sailor from Denison, and he was coming home on leave. He had a friend, also a sailor, who needed a date. I wouldn't consider it at first, and Wyonne thought she persuaded me. Actually, I persuaded myself, thinking how lovely it would feel to be inside one of those cars that circled the Square on Saturday nights, safe from the raucous remarks of cruising young males who pounded on their car doors as they drove.

Wyonne went with me to the telephone office to talk to Mom about it, and that was a mistake. First of all, Mom didn't like to have me bother her at work. And second, the very sight of Wyonne was a spark striking tinder in Mom. Before I'd even explained what we wanted, Mom was tightening her mouth.

"What's the matter, Mrs. Langelund?" Wyonne said. "Don't you trust Margaret?"

"It's not Margaret I don't trust."

"But Duane's father is a preacher—a Baptist preacher."

"That settles it. The answer is no."

"But why?" I yelped.

"Number, please."

When it was time for Mom to come home from work, I positioned myself on the front steps and tried to look tragic. She sighed, put down the bag of groceries from the A & P, and sat on the step beside me.

"This isn't your one and only chance to go out on a date, you know."

"Yes, it is! If I'm going to have a date, it has to be somebody from out of town. The guys here think I'm peculiar because I read and practice clarinet all the time."

"Wyonne will do things she shouldn't, and you'll think you have to do likewise."

"With a preacher's kid?"

"Especially with a preacher's kid. They cut their teeth on *don'ts,* and when they find something their parents are too embarrassed to mention, they have at it."

"But *I* wouldn't, Mom, even if it's something you never told me I couldn't do. Please, don't ruin my life."

She looked at me steadily for a long moment and then said, "You have so much to learn that I suppose you might as well begin. All right, you can go out with this Duane."

My fierce hug knocked over the groceries. I chased a rolling onion with joy before I ran all the way to Wyonne's house to tell her the good news. Max was home from medical school for the weekend, and this was the first time he had seen me since my operation. He whistled.

"It that you, Margaret?" he said.

"It's me."

Max was thin and sallow from long hours of study. I marveled that I'd ever loved him and couldn't resist rewarding his new interest with the news that I was going out with a sailor.

"Fasten your figleaf, the fleet's in," he said nastily.

Fortunately I wasted no more time on Max and got to Wyonne just as she was going to the phone to find another date for Duane.

The week crept toward Saturday like an inchworm. Exhausted by alternating anticipation and dread, I was dressed and waiting an hour ahead of time. Hair washed in rain water and rinsed with vinegar gleamed and bounced. Waves of valley lily scent rose from a wad of cotton thrust into my bra. An apple-green dress of Marianne's had been let out to its limits to span my hips, and I wished I could trim those hips with a meat cleaver. If I kept my coat on most of the time, Duane might not notice their size.

What if he didn't like me? What if he did and wanted to kiss me? Should I wipe off my lipstick first? Members of our family seldom kissed each other on the mouth, and I wasn't sure how it was done. That quick brush with Roger hadn't taught me much. I was practicing on the back of my hand when the phone rang.

"They had a flat tire, and it's a good thing," Wyonne said. "I'm not half ready. Why in heck can't we have the same phone? I had to put my coat on over my slip to call you from the Kepharts'."

The added delay gave me a carsick feeling. I hung up and rubbed my clammy palms, wondering if I should dust them with talcum powder. No, the Cashmere Bouquet would fight with my valley lily cologne. How could Wyonne be so casual—half-dressed five minutes before the appointed hour?

Mom suggested that I read for awhile, and I tried, but I eyed the same paragraph over and over without the slightest knowledge of what it said. Every time a car slowed outside, I tensed and reached for coat and purse. When a horn honked insistently, I sprang to my feet.

"It's them!"

Mom pushed me back into the chair. "Let them come to the door for you."

The horn sounded again. I was frantic. Then Wyonne hurried inside without knocking. Her red dress matched her Revlon mouth exactly.

"What's holding you up?"

"I'd like to meet your friends," Mom said.

I groaned and Wyonne rolled her eyes, but she went out on the porch and yelled at the sailors. They stood for inspection under the porch light, holding their tightly-rolled sailor caps in their hands. They were the same height (not tall), but whereas Gene was slender and lazy-eyed, Duane was rounded and earnest. The uniform made them look like boy dolls, and that's probably why Mom smiled to herself when she told us to have a good time.

Duane put me into the back seat and came around to sit close to the opposite window.

"How about going to Atlantic?" Wyonne said.

"Can't," Gene told her. "I've got just enough gas to get home, and I took that from the old man's tractor. What's on at the show?"

"I've seen it. Let's buy some beer and go out to Rabbit Hollow."

I caught my breath sharply. Brewing beer in the kitchen was one thing, but buying it in wicked, brown bottles in a dark tavern was something else. Also, girls who allowed themselves to be taken to the winding road through Rabbit Hollow were trash. I looked to Duane, the preacher's kid, for rescue.

"I'll have Pabst," he said. "What's yours?"

"The same," I said, hating him. I had imagined this first date as a meeting with someone who would recognize the real self I didn't have the courage to reveal. Duane was no help.

It was warm for October, but I was shivering. I pushed my feet hard against the floor of the car to hide the state I was in, but there was nothing I could do about the tremor in my voice when I questioned Duane about boot camp. He answered in monosyllables.

Gene parked in front of Herman's Tap on the Square and went inside to buy the beer. I was terrified that someone I knew would see me. As Gene was coming out with his bottles, Mary Lois Engle walked past. She was so goggle-eyed at the sight of a sailor that I couldn't resist rolling the window down and calling to her. Suddenly it didn't seem so terrible to be observed outside Herman's Tap.

"Why, Margaret," she said in what she thought was her Kathryn Grayson voice. "I didn't know you dated servicemen. In fact, I didn't know you dated. Aren't you going to introduce your friend?"

I presented Duane, and Mary Lois showed her dimples. She was Corliss Archer now. For the first time in my life, I had something she did not despise.

Wyonne was tired of being ignored. She said, "Slim pickings tonight? It's pretty late to be on foot, isn't it?"

"I just came uptown on an errand for my mother."

"What you're looking for, your mother doesn't need. Let's move it, Gene."

We burned rubber pulling away. I turned to look at Mary Lois through the back window, and the expression on her face more than made up for her taunts about the lines in my hands and my black tree trunks.

At a well-worn turnoff in Rabbit Hollow, we parked under the oak trees. The beer was bitter, and it gave me a pain in my shoulder.

Could that be the location of the conscience, I wondered? When Gene and Wyonne left the car to wander into the trees, Duane and I didn't know what to say to each other. The sweating beer bottle numbed my hand, and I wished I were at home listening to "Your Hit Parade." Duane took my bottle and tossed it and his into the underbrush.

"We don't have to pretend now, do we?"

"I didn't know you were."

"I figured you to be like Wyonne, but you're not. I'm not like Gene, either, but being in the Navy teaches you to act like one of those lizards that change color to match whatever they're sitting on. Know what I mean?"

"I think so, but I can't do it. I stay the same color and don't fool anybody."

"That's O.K., you're a nice color."

He touched my hair, and we kissed slowly and tentatively. It was much better than the time with Roger. I shivered with pleasure, which was better than shivering from sheer nervousness.

"Are you cold?"

"Yes and no."

I scrunched down to rest my cheek against the rough serge of his uniform, and when a sudden glare of headlights burst upon us, Duane covered my face with his cap, staring into the lights with the calm confidence of an anonymous out-of-towner. Then we kissed again, and I asked him to tell me what he was like when he was little.

"I worried about sin a lot. Dad's a brimstone preacher."

"Do you still?"

"No, I've got it all doped out. You don't have to earn brownie points to keep out of hell because Christ took care of all that. If you do right, it's because you're grateful, and if you don't, it's not fatal. The bill has been paid."

"That's the best sermon I ever heard," I said, meaning it, but Duane thought I was making fun of him and backed off. I searched for his hand in unspoken apology, bringing him close for another beery kiss.

"Hey," he said, "want some Sen-Sen? I always carry it because of Dad—not that it fools him."

We sucked the tiny, pungent pillows and talked until Wyonne and Gene came out of the woods.

"What have you two been doing?" Wyonne asked archly.

"Getting acquainted," Duane said.

She laughed, picking leaf bits and twigs from Gene's big, square collar. "That's one way of putting it."

Duane and I agreed to write to each other, and we parted with a long, Sen-Sen kiss.

Mom was awake in the dark house. She called to me, asking if I had a nice time, and I smiled to myself, running a finger over my transformed lips.

"Margaret, did you hear me?"

"Yes, I had a nice time. I didn't know what to do or say, but he made it all right."

Moving On

from *Amalie's Story*

[24]

I STAYED IN THE HOUSE the whole of that winter. The older girls did the necessary shopping and Stig took care of Holger, who was growing fat and torpid in his stall in the carriage house. Stig begged to ride him, but I would not allow it.

My days were taken up by the care of Petra, rubbing oil into the furniture, tending my house plants, and cooking all the dishes Mor used to make.

Much virtue attached to visiting widows and orphans in their affliction, and my front door opened daily to the curious and the truly sympathetic. I found the former easier to bear, for I could make a game of withholding the things they wanted to know.

"What will happen to the Beehive?" Mrs. Nicolai asked.

"What has always happened, I suppose."

"You mean you will retain your interest in it?"

"Det bliver min sag," I replied with a shrug, and Mrs. Nicolai didn't dare to press for the translation—"That's my affair."

"Mr. Nicolai told me to ask if you would like to sell Holger," she said. "We'd like to help in any way we can."

"Thank you, but I will keep Holger. He is a friend."

"Well, since you sold the carriage horses, I thought you might be in need—"

I smiled enigmatically.

"Well," she sniffed, "it's nice that you can afford to be so independent. You do have five children to raise, you know."

"I know," I said, smiling at Petra asleep in her longskirted basket.

The visit was cut short by the return of Valborg and Else from an ice-skating party on the Nishnabotna. Their cheeks were red as

Graasten apples, and they wore their skates into the kitchen, having found a run of ice all the way from the river to our house.

"They'll cut up your floors!" Mrs. Nicolai gasped.

"They'll be off again as soon as they're warm," I said indulgently, "it's a lot of bother to unstrap."

Mrs. Nicolai went off shaking her head, and I was left to muse about the alteration in my house pride. Now I kept up the other rooms better than I ever had done, but the kitchen was the room where we lived, and there were no rules or restrictions there. Anyone who was sick reclined on a daybed along the south wall. A big, hinged chest held the toys of the younger children. My set of Dickens was stacked in a corner against the day when I might take enough interest in human experience to read again.

Just now, it was enough to watch the sun's rays bend through the wavy glass of the windows and listen to the shrill voice of the teakettle pulled to the front burner for the company of its whistle. Once the first racking grief was past, life without Peter was a plateau of uneventful existence. I seldom knew what day it was, and when the children turned a leaf of the calendar to a new month, I was without regret or anticipation.

Until they begged me to put their long underwear away, I had no notion that spring had come. I stepped into the yard to test the temperature and saw the young grape leaves uncurling on the vines of the arbor. The breeze carried the bitter-sweet scent of the prairie's greening.

"You may change to muslin," I said, leaving the back door ajar as I came in.

With wild whoops they ran to their rooms to shed the cumbersome, baggy garments that had imprisoned them for months. When I next saw them, they were slimmer and more graceful—butterflies freed from the essential but ugly chrysalis. The change forced me to look at them more carefully than I had for months.

Valborg had ripened, not to beauty, but to a healthy attractiveness. She was in love for what would be the first of many times. I should have listened more carefully when she told me about the boy, because I searched for his name and could not find it.

Else had grown vain—with cause. She loved chiefly herself, and the sheer arrogance of that regard forced unwilling admiration from others.

Kamille was all eyes and angles, a dreamer who gave common things the lustre of imagination. She was forever telling Stig about Papa's activities in heaven, inventing a house for Peter, angel friends, and a business of selling the goods for celestial robes. One would think she had been dipping into my Swedenborg, but that could not be. Turned against it by Lily, I had packed the book away in the crawl space above the trap door in our bedroom.

And there was Stig, so often willful and stubborn, just coming into the years when a boy needs a man to imitate. I had let him run with companions I did not know all winter, and the spring blooming of my neglect was filthy language and small cruelties, which he brought home in all innocence. That innocence disarmed me, and I reproved but did not punish. Stig was so beguiling in easy repentance.

"Stay in the yard, Stig," I said as the three girls went off to school.

"Can't I go to Lily's?" he begged.

"Well, just for a little while."

Petra was crowing and kicking in the beechwood cradle. She had outgrown the fancy, skirted basket that had been the gift of Lily and John.

"What will you be?" I asked, smiling into her elfish little face. She laughed out loud.

As I went about opening the windows to spring, I felt the restlessness of long confinement for the first time. I had been so much with my children that I could no longer see them clearly. It was time to walk out of this house, if only for a little while.

I bundled Petra into a shawl and crossed the street to Lily's back door. Stig was enjoying a stack of cookies and a glass of milk at Lily's kitchen table, and he did not seem pleased at the prospect of sharing his Lady Bountiful.

On sudden impulse, I said, "Lily, will you take care of these two for a little while? I think I'll saddle Holger and ride."

"That's a marvelous idea!" she said, reaching for Petra. "I was beginning to wonder if you would ever come out of it."

"I'm not sure I want to—it's comfortable to be numb—but spring won't let me stay that way. The children are out of their union suits, and well . . ." I shrugged, laughing.

Holger puffed his sides and wheezed a complaint as I cinched him tightly. I had rejected my own sidesaddle for Peter's, but I could not pull the strap to the well-worn notch he had used. Holger was fatter and I was weaker. This was just one more instance of being unable to take Peter's place, but I would try, riding astride in his saddle.

A stray dog was enough to make Holger shy after a long, cozy idleness in his stall, and I took the quickest route out of town. The prairie, which once bordered our first house by the mill, had given way to cultivated land. I saw farmers walking behind the steel self-scouring plows that made the breaking of the prairie possible. The black-brown earth parted before the blade, falling away like scoops of hand-cranked ice cream. Something in my Jutland heart rejoiced at the cultivation, but something new and possibly American yearned for prairie untouched by man. I rode far enough to find it and urged Holger to a wild gallop through tall grasses, dead and brown at the level where they brushed my saddle-divided skirt, but green far below, where spring was working its miracle.

Whipped from his lethargy, Holger was exhilarated by that great, free space, and he tried to shake the bit from his teeth when I turned him back toward town.

"We're only free for a little while," I said, leaning forward to slap him on the neck affectionately.

As I rode back into town on Sixth Street, I passed Edward Parmeter in his one-seater. He seemed surprised to see me and stared pointedly at my unsuitable dress and saddle.

"May I call tomorrow?" he asked.

"Of course." After I said it, I wished I hadn't, but my reluctance to see Edward was ridiculous. After all, he had handled all the business matters after Peter's death, and I should be grateful to him.

When Edward arrived, I was waiting in a black broadcloth dress too heavy for the weather. The breeze that billowed the parlor curtains was languorously warm, and I cooled myself with the Spanish fan Far had given me on my confirmation day.

"Are you speaking to me in the language of the fan, Amalie?" he asked.

This was the first time he had used my given name, and both the address and the question flustered me.

"I doubt that such language is of use in talking business," I answered, folding the fan.

"Something must be done about the partnership, of course, but perhaps we can come to a solution that will embrace more than business. By the way, is your clutch of children likely to pop from behind the settee? I had hoped for a private conversation."

"You shall have it," I said curtly, refusing to volunteer the fact that we were alone in the house. I sat down on the settee and straightened my back primly, folding my hands in my black lap.

"I hadn't meant to speak to you so soon," he said, "but when I saw you out riding like a hoyden, I realized I had misjudged your sense of the niceties."

"How can you talk to me that way?" I cried, amazed at my degree of hurt. I had experienced no feeling so sharp in more than half a year.

"I'm sorry," he said, taking my hand, "that was harsh, but your reaction told me what I needed to know. You do feel something for me."

"No! It's shocking that you should—"

His lips were hard on mine. The hands I raised to push him away seemed to have a will of their own, spreading to press his chest and shoulder in passionate exploration. I could not think. It was like the time with Birch Sandahl in the wood. I could not break from Edward, and when he released me, I turned from him, horrified at myself.

"Please go, I am ashamed!"

"You needn't be. Nothing stands in our way now."

"But I don't like you, Edward!" I said between clenched teeth, "I never have!"

"Liking is for friends," he said. "We are something else."

"Buy Peter's share in the Beehive from me and leave me alone!"

"I can't. Since Peter died, business has fallen off, and I don't have the money."

"Borrow it from John Hertert," I said, frightened by the implications of what he had told me.

"Be sensible, Amalie; the obvious solution to the whole problem is for us to marry, though I confess that I can't quite see myself as a paterfamilias."

"Get out!" I screamed, sickened by the impossible longing for him that survived even this cold-blooded proposition.

He stood and took his hat from the cane-seated chair that had been my mother's. "Madame, I apologize. I deeply regret your attitude, for aside from the financial soundness of my plan, I had looked forward to possessing you."

"Slange!" I shouted, too agitated to use English.

He bowed, smiled, and left me, not knowing that I had called him a snake.

Snake! Snake! Snake! The word rang with the echo of the front door's slamming. A snake on the misty Danish heath, a snake in the musty dampness of the root cellar on the farm, a snake that had entered and left this house with coil and thrust.

Birch Sandahl, Berg Landsman, Edward Parmeter. Why did my mind group them? I paced, pressing my clasped hands hard against my breastbone, shaking my head in a horrified denial of a question that demanded an answer.

"Oh, God, don't let the children come home yet!" I said aloud, and the sound of my voice frightened me. I went to the kitchen and tried to make a pot of coffee, but my hands shook too fiercely to measure and pour.

The question was written on the walls, on the shaft of afternoon sun that slanted through the window, on the pickets of the fence around the house.

What am I?

"Mor! Mother!" The cry burst from me with all the anguish of the moment of death, and I sat back drained, no longer fighting the question or its answer.

I saw my mother. Bodil and a faceless pastor walked on the heath, and as they went deeper into the moor, I felt the coursing of her blood, the mindless power that had moved my hands over Edward Parmeter's shoulders.

I had blamed her for succumbing to that power, for being deafened to the whisper of conscience by the roar of her blood; blamed her and buried the deed so deep that I never expected to think of it again.

No one would ever know how close I had come to yielding to Edward. If a widow of thirty-five, with six living children, could feel such engulfing temptation, what of a girl of sixteen?

I knew her now as I never had known her before, and it was too late to tell her so. My blood was her blood; a bequest not to be despised, for it had been my gift to Peter—the first helping of my heart.

My hands stopped shaking, and I made the coffee.

John Hertert took over my business affairs; at Lily's insistence, I suspected. I had no need to see Edward, but when a few months had passed, I was strong enough to walk into the Beehive, greet him, and make a purchase. I knew myself now, and his gaze no longer had the power to confound me.

I came home to find the younger children playing dominoes at the kitchen table. When they clamored for my old fairy tale, "Amalie's Story," I told it. "But you must remember," I said, "the story isn't true."

"We know, Mama," Kamille said, "but we like it anyhow."

from *Petra*

[20]

THE DRIFTERS CAME THAT SUMMER. I gave eggs and milk to anyone who asked. We were getting two cents a quart for our milk, and it cost money to haul it to town, but Lauritz refused to dump it.

"Someone always comes to drink it. I will not waste good food!"

The slaughter of baby pigs that went on all around us sickened me. Ours were allowed to live and root for food in the timber, reverting to a wild state.

"What are you going to do with them in the winter?" Cliff Potter asked.

"Butcher what we need and give the rest away."

"You won't dump, you won't slaughter, you won't march on Washington—" Cliff said in exasperation, "you're just not doing a damned thing to help!"

"I refuse to be afraid. That helps."

Cliff stalked away, angry, but he was to remember Lauritz's words when he heard Franklin Delano Roosevelt's radio voice intoning: "We have nothing to fear but fear itself!"

Prices rose in the summer of 1933, but we couldn't benefit until the crops were harvested. We endured the hot, dry summer, wondering if there would be anything to harvest.

Cliff Potter gave up and went to California. Things weren't much better there, he wrote back. The roads were clogged by midwestern emigrants and the famous climate was marred by smoke from fired mountains of kerosene-soaked oranges.

Lauritz finished the bridge across the south pasture gully and whipped Willy and Fritz into trotting across it. They were frightened by the rumbling boards, but they were more frightened of Lauritz.

They didn't have to suffer the crossings for long, for when they had hauled the last load of corn across the bridge, Lauritz sold them and bought a John Deere tractor.

I held Margaret high to watch the mules make their surly way down the lane for the last time. "There they go, the nasty things!" I said happily. I resisted the urge to throw a clod after them.

Lauritz was quiet and thoughtful when he returned from delivering Willy and Fritz to their new owner.

"Don't tell me you miss those monsters!"

He smiled wryly. "The tractor won't be as much company. I was used to them."

They brought the tractor the next day. I took Margaret out to admire its green and yellow glory, and she drew back, seemingly afraid of the machine. When Lauritz swung into the seat and held out his arms for her, she shook her head.

"Isn't it pretty, Margaret?" I tried to encourage her.

"Grasshopper!" she said.

Margaret was terrified of the hoppers that jumped on her bare legs and spurred her tender skin. She hated the acrid "tobacco" they spat on her.

"No, Margaret—tractor. It will help Daddy do his work faster so he can play with you more."

She remained unmollified, and I took her back to the house feeling sorry for Lauritz. He was so proud of his new machine, and Margaret's rejection of it must have hurt.

The black blizzard in South Dakota on Armistice Day was fully reported in the papers. Some people interpreted it as a sign of Divine displeasure. Lauritz read the accounts aloud to me, and we shook our heads over the wall of black dirt that hid the sun—the drifts higher than a man—and the black deposits that people brought up from their lungs.

"It's because we've mistreated the land," he said. "I've done it myself with that ditch in the south pasture. It's eating the field away."

"You still have more usable land than before—"

"Not for long. That ditch is hungry!"

"Oh well, we have other fields."

That winter was piercingly cold. We had used all the dead wood on the place, and the money we might have spent for fuel was tied up in the tractor.

"You don't play the organ anymore," Lauritz said.

"I will when spring warms the parlor."

"Would you miss it terribly?"

"Lauritz, you wouldn't!"

"Better that than something useful."

"But I want it for Margaret!"

"She won't be able to reach the pedals for years, and by then, things will be better. I'll buy her a piano."

"Would you trade years of pleasure for a few hours of heat?"

He inclined his head toward Margaret, who was entangled with Sofus on the floor close to the kitchen stove. She wore two sweaters, her fingers were a mottled mulberry, and her nose ran.

"All right," I said with a sigh, "go ahead."

He brought the hatchet from the shed. When he opened the door to the frigid parlor, I hastily put on my coat and went outside. I couldn't bear to hear the blows. I walked to the end of the lane to check the mailbox. Empty.

Through the long harshness of want, I never had given up on beauty. I embroidered plain sheets for bedspreads when the old ones wore out. I grew nasturtiums below the south windows from a jar of carefully hoarded seeds. I played my simple triads, hearing better music in my head.

I gazed over the frozen fields, obscurely blaming them for taking something precious from me. We were rich enough to have a tractor and too poor to have an organ. Everything went to the land!

But the organ gave one last burst of beauty. When I came back to the house, Margaret was standing before the isinglass panels of the dining room stove, enraptured by dancing orange flames.

In the winter of 1934, Cliff and Anna Potter came back from California. The women of the neighborhood cleaned their house, which had stood empty in their absence, and the men sanded rust from their abandoned farm machinery.

"Things are going to get better now," Cliff said, "and I can't abide a place where the seasons don't turn."

It was good to have close neighbors again. I bundled Margaret into her wraps and walked up the hill to drink coffee with Anna in the late afternoon.

"That child sure likes to sit around with grown-ups," Anna observed. "Most of 'em can't get away from us quick enough!"

"We've never used baby talk with her."

"Nice that you two can agree about raising a young'un. Me and Cliff had different ideas, and the kids sort of fell between."

I didn't tell Anna, but Lauritz and I were less in harmony about the rearing of Margaret than she supposed. Lauritz roared when Margaret played with her food, but I was inclined to indulge her in this if she could be induced to eat at all. He gave her chores I considered too heavy for a tiny girl, such as carrying buckets of mash to the chickens.

One day she walked barefoot across a deceptively gray bed of ashes in a burned-out ditch and dropped a kitten she was carrying on the concealed coals. Lauritz was cutting tree limbs nearby. Hearing the cries of the kitten, he rushed to the rescue.

When I saw him thrashing Margaret with a thin switch, I ran out shouting, "What are you doing?"

"She lied to me!" He was breathing hard, radiating a dark rage. "Said a strange man came down the road and threw her kitten in the fire, but I saw it all. She dropped that cat!" He picked up the struggling bit of fur and showed me its blistered footpads.

I gathered up the weeping Margaret, fierce as any mother lion in the face of harm to her cub. "Have you looked at *her* feet?"

He nodded disgustedly. "She was quick enough to save herself!"

"You can't blame her! It hurt, and she was scared."

"That's no excuse for a lie."

"Daddy's mean!" Margaret said, pointing pitifully to the welts on her legs.

Lauritz turned away, wounded, and I hurt him more by saying, "I'd hate to be the kind of person who makes a child afraid to tell the truth."

We didn't see him for the rest of the day. My righteousness ebbed as I tied the kitten on its back in a shoe box and greased its burned paws with unsalted butter.

Reluctantly I asked Margaret, "Did you drop the kitty?"

"No."

I went looking for Lauritz and found him mending a section of the hogpen fence. He went on hammering as if he didn't know I was there.

"Lauritz, I was wrong. We shouldn't take sides when Margaret misbehaves. But where could she have learned to lie? She never sees anybody but us—"

"Man is born unto evil, as the sparks fly upward—"

"Don't quote things. We're talking about our child!"

"Who is no angel from heaven!"

"She is to me!" Then, realizing I was prolonging the quarrel, I stopped his hammer in midswing. "Lauritz, if you really have to punish her, be gentler. I don't want her to hate you."

"Do you think she does?"

"No, of course not," I said, though I wasn't sure.

Margaret ate her supper without tunneling through her mashed potatoes, and when Lauritz pushed back from the table, she climbed on his lap to tie his hair in knots, laughing up at him with unclouded joy. Or was it unclouded? Her determined coquettishness had a strained urgency about it.

Fridays brought an expectation of surprises: a trip to town on the following day, weekend visitors, a break from fieldwork. Margaret loved the Friday feeling and so did I.

April 13 fell on a Friday in that spring of 1934, and my heritage of Danish superstition was strong enough to make me look at the calendar with a slight shiver. I denied the qualm, humming as I made breakfast.

"Where are you working today, Lauritz?"

"I'm going across the bridge to plow. We'll see how well the grasshopper pulls a blade."

We kissed at the door, and I raised Margaret for the triple nose rubbing that delighted her.

"If you'll wait a minute, we'll get our coats and walk you to the barn—"

"Stay in where it's warm. It's raw out, and I'll be glad to come in for dinner."

I washed the breakfast dishes while Margaret slid around the kitchen floor in one of my long black bread pans. It was her Ford. It didn't rain, but the air was heavy, and I slowly lost my enthusiasm for the Friday cleaning. Putting aside my dustcloth, I read 'Andy Gump' to Margaret. She loved the chinless fellow.

"Oh, Min!" I read, trying again for a more impressive inflection, "Oh, Min!"

"Petra!"

It sounded like Cliff Potter outside, and I heard him so clearly that I wondered whether the kitchen door had blown open.

"Read!" Margaret demanded.

"In a minute, Honey, I have to see what Cliff wants—"

Cliff was fumbling with a gate latch as familiar to him as his own. When he saw me, he stopped, looking at me across the distance with an anguish that terrified me. "Anna saw it through the window—she's coming—"

I rushed to unfasten the gate, pushing past him.

"No, Petra! You can't go down there!" He caught my arms and held me while I fought, not caring that I hurt him. I had to get to the bridge!

"Lauritz!" I screamed, "Lauritz!"

"Don't!" Cliff pleaded. "Anna's coming—she'll know what to say—do—"

"What's happened to Lauritz?"

"The bridge fell in. Anna looked out the window—saw the smoke and Sofus lying there looking down—"

A thin column of smoke still rose, straight as a plumb line. Men were looking over the edge of the gully, scrambling down its sides, and there was Sofus, his tawny coat a bright, still spot in that tangle of moving figures.

"The preacher's down there and the doctor's on the way—"

"Let me go, Cliff! I *have* to see him—"

"No!"

Then Anna was there, and the two of them held me.

"All those people knew, and I didn't—I was reading the funny papers."

One figure moved away from the others on the bank and came toward us. It was Reverend Wiuff, and I knew. While there was life, he had stayed. I sobbed out loud, making it impossible for him to tell me what I already knew. Margaret came outside, coatless and bewildered. Part of me knew I was frightening her with my wild grief, but I couldn't stop the deep, tearing sobs.

Throwing off the hands that held me, I ran into the windbreak, throwing myself from one tree trunk to the next in mindless pain.

"God! Why did you let this happen to someone who loved You and served You? He was young and strong and good! You've made a terrible mistake!"

The pastor started toward me, stepping carefully through the trees. I turned him back with raised clenched fists. "Don't come near me! I don't want you or your God!"

"You need *your* God!"

"I need Lauritz! Get away from me." I pounded my forehead on the trunk of a young tree until the blood ran down into my eyes, but I stayed conscious—wretchedly conscious.

I whirled, snarling at the touch on my arm, and Doctor Gus yelled, "Damn it, Petra, stand still!" He rammed a hypodermic needle into my arm and withdrew it before I knew what had happened. "If it's any comfort to you, he suffered four minutes at the outside, and not a bone in his body was broken."

"Four minutes—how—"

"The tractor flipped and the fender caught him in the back—pushed his face in the dirt. Suffocation. Now you know. You don't have to imagine anything."

I stared at the old man who had slapped me into life and wished that he hadn't. Whatever was in that needle numbed me, filled my head with a high singing. I held out my other arm.

"Do it again. Give me enough to die!"

"Don't be a fool! Who'd take care of Margaret?"

Margaret! I'd forgotten all about her for the first time since her birth.

"You'd better get into the house and lie down before you fall down," he said gruffly. "Your mother's on the way. She'll know what to do with you."

As we came out of the trees, the long black hearse from Pauley's went past, jouncing grotesquely along the rutted path to the south field. I watched, as detached as if it had nothing to do with me, and when Karl's car swerved up on the grassy bank to give it room, I thought of the ugly tire marks he would leave on the slope.

Mama called my name, and I tried to run to her, but the shot had made my legs too heavy. I stood where I was, holding out my arms and wailing like a child younger than Margaret.

"Lille Petra—" She pulled me close, but there was too much of me for her to hold. "This is the worst moment you will ever know. Come—"

I dragged myself after her to the house, noticing how her once-straight back was bent. Her carmel hair had grayed and thinned until the meager knot would scarcely hold its tortoise shell pins. She was ravaged by time but still alive, while Lauritz—my loss struck me freshly like a sudden wave of nausea.

"The worst moment," she had said. No. A moment began and ended, but this would be forever. I saw Mama holding the door for me as I lost consciousness.

I woke in another day, confused but not unhappy until I remembered Mama's voice reading "Andy Gump" to Margaret in the next room brought it all back. She heard me stirring and came to the door. "Get dressed, Petra."

Karl came to drive us to town, and we debated whether Margaret should see Lauritz at the funeral home.

"No," I said, "let her remember him as he was."

"He looks real natural," Karl said. "Nothing to scare her."

"Natural? Life is natural to Lauritz—nothing else!"

"She should see him and know," Mama said. "Otherwise she'll think he went away and left her."

"Then you'll have to take her in. I can't."

They had him in a bed, dressed in his best dark blue suit and covered to the waist with a horrible pink jacquard spread. The deep lines between his brows were filled with waxy makeup and I leaned down to gouge it out with my fingernail. Then he looked as if he were sleeping, dressed for church.

I had bought a wedding ring for him, fourteen years late, meaning to give it to him for his birthday, even if he could wear it only on Sundays. Rings were dangerous for a man working with farm machinery. I took it from my purse and forced it on his stiff finger. Then I breathed on it to cloud its awful brightness, giving it a temporary patina of the years of wear that would not be.

"Good-bye, my dearest love, I'll see you in the morning." I did not kiss his lips, letting the warm kiss of an April morning be our last. My life would be a long, gray tunnel to the morning of our next. I had read in the Bible that in heaven there would be no marrying or giving in marriage, but surely the good marriages made on earth would not be broken.

I left him in that room heavy with the scent of roses, burning to get through my life quickly and join him. When I heard Margaret's voice saying, "Does Daddy have his shoes on in bed?" I remembered that my existence was joined to hers, and she was heartbreakingly young. She would have need of me for a long, long time.

Mama stayed with me for the next five months. We made an odd sort of couple—with her caring for Margaret and the house while

I worked in the fields to finish the spring planting.

The neighbors helped to the point of neglecting their own fields until I realized I would have to hire help. I went to town to interview hired men and was so disgusted by the poor quality of the applicants that I came home with no prospects.

"Didn't you find one strong back?" Mama asked.

"Just one, and he looked at me in a way I couldn't stand. When they know you're a widow with land, they get ideas."

"What was wrong with the others?"

"Bindlestiffs with hookworm and the rickets. I doubt they could do a day's work."

"Try again tomorrow. Maybe you can find somebody in Audubon."

I hired a man there, the first of five, and he went to the hospital for an appendicitis operation before he had been with us a week.

The replacement waited two weeks before he asked me to marry him, and when I refused, he became so surly that I had to ask him to leave. His name was Bink Souder, and he had a cast in one eye. His good eye was on the land. Souder's successor cut the roots of the corn when he plowed, and I discovered much too late that he had lied to me about his agricultural experience. The next one slapped Margaret when she interrupted his nap under a shade tree by tickling his nose with a foxtail weed.

The last one offered the second proposal of my bereavement and was, I think, sincere. Marriage was unthinkable to me, and besides, I couldn't stand the sight of him. The top of his head came to my shoulder; the throat of his shirt was choked with black, curly hair; and his mouth was slack and damp. His name was Lester Kincaid. No matter how a woman feels about the men who propose to her, it's only courteous for her to remember their names.

I didn't feel much like a woman that year or for a long time after. I no longer slept in the bed Lauritz and I had shared. The imprint of his body was in the mattress, and to roll into that slight hollow made me burn with a need that could never be satisfied. A narrow couch pained me less. It deceived me into thinking I was a girl again; a young girl with no knowledge of touching and fusing.

All that summer I struggled to raise a crop and finish stock for the market, despairing over broken machinery, veterinary bills, and the proliferation of burdocks, the sure mark of a bad farmer.

In September Margaret began to walk the mile to the country schoolhouse. I never had time to ask her much about school—no more than a hasty "How was it?" as I hurried to the barn to milk.

She didn't volunteer much either, but I thought little of it because she had grown very quiet since Lauritz's death. One day when she came down the lane swinging her lunch bucket, I called to her, "Come and talk to me while I slop the hogs, Margaret."

She came running, stumbled, and fell. The catch of her lunch bucket flew open, and everything Mama had packed for her that morning spilled out on the ground.

"Why didn't you eat your lunch?" I asked, brushing off her knees and blowing a kiss toward each skinny knob.

She shrugged, turning at the sound of a car in the lane.

"It's your teacher, Miss Keppy."

Margaret streaked off to the outhouse and shut the bolt inside.

Miss Keppy came toward me with a harried smile. "Mrs. Langelund, I hate to bother you in your sorrow, but—"

"Is Margaret having trouble in school?"

"No, that is—she hasn't *been* to school for two weeks. The children tell me she spends the day with Mrs. Anderson and starts for home when she sees the others go by."

"But why?"

"I thought maybe you'd know that."

I flushed with shame. I hadn't spent ten minutes with Margaret in the past two weeks, and I had no idea what she was thinking or feeling.

"I'll find out, Miss Keppy, and she'll be in school tomorrow."

Margaret would neither come out of the outhouse nor let me in.

"You don't need to be afraid of me. I'm not going to punish you. Why don't you let me help make things right?"

"You can't," came the muffled reply.

"I can!"

"Not like Daddy could've!"

I pressed my forearm hard against my eyes to hold back the tears. "Margaret, Daddy isn't here—so whatever it is, I'll have to take care of it. Now what *is* the matter?"

I waited, and after a long time, she said, "The big boys hit me and push me down at recess." The door remained bolted.

"Did you tell Miss Keppy?"

"No, they're bigger than she is."

"Do they hit the other little children?"

"They've got big brothers and sisters."

"Not Betty Waring."

"They don't hit her 'cause her daddy came to school and sat in a desk all day. He even went out to recess."

"I can do that." I had grown so angry that the rough grain of the door swam before my eyes. The Cletus Bunkers of Tyler School Number Two were not going to torment *my* child!

The next day I took Margaret to school and stayed, taking an eighth grade desk in the back near the water bucket. Observing the young, inexperienced Miss Keppy, I knew that I could step to the front of the room and take over. The curriculum had not changed since my first year at Jackson Number Three. The children could learn so little in the brief minutes the teacher could spare for each grade. Margaret should have something better.

At recess, I played ring-around-the-rosie with the smallest girls, and Margaret refused to take my hand in the circle. When it was time for lunch, I found a grassy slope, sat down, and opened my shoebox of sandwiches, pears, and cookies, thinking Margaret would come to me, but she and Betty Waring plunked their bright lunch buckets tantalizingly close to the eighth grade boys. When one of them hit Margaret with a plum pit, she retrieved it and fired it back. The boy thumbed his nose at her, turning furtively to see if I had noticed.

At the end of the day that same boy brushed past Margaret, muttering, "Mama's baby! I'll get you when she ain't around!"

Margaret's hand found mine as she stuck her tongue out.

Walking through the fine-sifted dust at the road edge, I despaired of a solution to Margaret's problem. I couldn't be with her all the time.

"Margaret, you deliberately provoked that boy."

"What's pervoke?"

I explained, and she seemed to listen, but when I stopped talking, she said, "I'm going to put chicken pooh in his lunch bucket tomorrow!"

"If you do, you'll have to take the consequences. Why in the world would you want to do that?"

"When I do something to him, he looks at me and yells, 'Cut that out, you dumb little shit!' "

I stopped, watching her trudge on, raising puffs of dust. When she realized she was alone, she turned.

"Never say that word again!"

"Which one?"

I couldn't repeat it, but she knew. I could tell by the way the light glanced from her deep blue irises. Mischief made them look like blue water lakes in the sun. To Lauritz, that look was prelude to the razor strop, but I had not punished her since he died.

"Margaret," I sighed, "I thought I understood why you stayed out of school—because the big boys were mean to you—but if you enjoy that, why did you go to Mrs. Anderson's?"

Her incomprehension was deliberate, I was sure, and I was losing my patience, which she knew. Just as I leaned down to break off a heavy weed stalk for a switch, she said, "When Bart talks, he sounds like Daddy, so I try to make him talk to me. He won't unless I make him mad, and then he hits me, but if I stay with Mrs. Anderson, I can holler at him when he goes by on the road. All he can do is holler back."

"I can't understand Mrs. Anderson letting you stay there all those days without telling me."

"I told her you didn't want me to go to school because of the mean boys, but everybody at home was too busy to take care of me."

"But she knows Grandma is here."

"I told her Grandma was sick."

"Margaret, you lied! You told one lie after another!"

"I had to! I wanted to hear Bart sound like Daddy and not get hurt."

My heart was wrung, but I broke the weed stalk with a snap and methodically switched those beautifully formed young legs.

"That's for lying."

I walked away from her, then came back to snatch her hand and drag her with me. She cried, and I wanted to, but I couldn't indulge myself.

Pulling her down the lane, I looked around me with despair. The harrow, broken and rusting, lay in tall weeds beside the barn, which needed paint. The hogs had scours and the cattle had ringworm. At least an acre of the nearest cornfield was bald from the rootcutting plowing.

I had failed the land that Lauritz's blood remembered, and I had failed his child, wailing at my side.

"Go in the house," I told Margaret, and I walked the fences of the nearest fields to let the full extent of the effects of my ruinous management sink in. As far as the land went, I was licked, but I wouldn't give up on Margaret!

Leaving the farm, I knew how divorce must make a woman feel. I remembered the early love for the land and wept at the bitter things it had done to me. The parting was cruel, and yet a relief.

Once more the furniture stood on the lawn; this time there was no one to buy and give back my marriage bed. Karl bought it for Jack Russell, who would bring his bride to a rented farm in a month's time. They were much too young to marry, but they loved each other, and the girl was pregnant.

I didn't go into the yard for the auction, but now and then I looked out the window at the auctioneer on his high stand. I turned away when the bidding on the green and yellow tractor started. It had not been damaged in the collapse of the bridge, and it brought a good price.

We came home to the blue house at dusk. Margaret had never slept in town, and whenever she heard a train whistle, she jumped up and ran to the window, expecting to see a locomotive in the street outside.

She turned her back to me in the feather bed, and when I tried to pull her close, she struggled out of the hollow and clung to the edge of the bed. Ah well, I was not my mother, and Margaret was not me.

I was back at the beginning—in a world without men. I yearned for the innocence that knew nothing else, despaired of regaining it, and knew finally that I could endure—as my mother had. It is the women who abide and maintain houses of refuge for those whose bridges have fallen.

from *The Sailing Out*

[28]

THE HIGH SCHOOL WAS only three blocks away, but we took the car, arriving at the same time as Mary Lois Engle and her date, a "better than nothing" escort.

It occurred to me that I hadn't mentioned our house guest to anyone, and I asked Davy, "Do you mind if I don't say you're my cousin?"

He laughed. "Tell 'em anything you please. I don't know a soul in this town anymore, so you'll never get caught."

Merrilee rushed over to greet us as we came into the gym, and I said, "This is Dave." Lotus, Monica, and Wyonne got the same cryptic introduction.

"Your dress is gorgeous," Wyonne whispered, "and so is he."

Davy was an excellent dancer—good enough to make me seem better than I was. He swept me through trellises of paper orchids, close to the bandstand, and past the mystified but smiling chaperones. It seemed that everyone was looking at us.

"Having a good time?" he asked.

"For once I *really* feel like Hedy Lamarr, but I suppose it isn't much fun for you."

"Sure it is. It takes me back. Maybe I should have married that girl I took to the senior prom."

We danced until the band played "Good-Night Sweetheart," but Davy drew the line at the postprom dinner in another town followed by an all-night party at the field club. I was perfectly willing to disappear like Cinderella before I was found out.

"I'll never forget this," I told him.

"Good," he said. "That's the idea."

"Whose idea was this?"

He laughed. "You know the Jorgen girls. They might seem as

practical as bacon and eggs, but they're romantics—every one of 'em. Come to think of it, that's a pretty good description of a Dane."

We sat in the car under the streetlight talking for awhile before we went in, and I confessed what I had done to Davy's snapshot image. Considering what he had done for me, I was sorry.

"Think nothing of it, kid. I'm not sure I'd want *my* mother to love anybody else the way Aunt Pete loved me—Uncle Lauritz, too. I owe a lot to both of them. Your dad was quite a man, Margaret. Too bad you lost him so soon."

"If we hadn't, maybe I'd be going to college."

"Don't let that stop you." He smacked a fist into his palm. "Get there, do you hear?"

"We don't have the money."

"Then beg, borrow, or steal it! Don't be like me—thinking you'll make some money first and then go. I've said that for years, but I never get around to it."

We found Mom and Grandma at the kitchen table drinking tea and waiting to hear all. Their eyes shone as we talked, and Davy laughed, saying, "What did I tell you? Romantics."

"Pshaw!" said Grandma, but she wasn't displeased.

We stayed up later than I'd ever been awake, even on New Year's Eve, and when we finally rose from the table yawning, Davy leaned down and kissed my forehead.

"Don't forget what I told you," he said.

The next day he climbed into the green Ford and headed for New Mexico. Mom and Grandma turned away well before the car was out of sight, but I took the risk of watching until only a sliver of green roof was visible above the Willow Street hill.

"What was it that Davy didn't want you to forget?" Mom asked.

"How much you and Daddy did for him," I said, not wanting to worry her with his expensive recommendation. No matter what Davy said, college was out of the question for me.

"We did love him like our own," she said, "and then you came along." She put her arm around me and gave me a hug.

I was watching Grandma, thinking that Davy and I had the same blood relationship with her, but he hadn't lived with her for as many years as I had. Now that he was gone, she was all mine again.

She caught my look and said, "Grandchildren are like books of the Bible—all precious and each special."

"Even the begats?" I said.

"Even the begats."

I walked to the law office humming "It Might As Well Be Spring," and it was. After a Friday night rain, the May morning glittered and dazzled. The lawns were as green as Easter basket grass. Rain had pooled in the waxy cups of late tulips, lapping at the dark anthers I had thought of as little people sitting around a table until a science teacher dashed my fancy.

This was the first day I had been allowed to leave the house in a cotton dress (the prom didn't count), and I felt reborn. My friends had been out of their winter cocoons all week, but Mom stepped outside every morning to test the air and said, "Wait another day." This was the day. It was nearly as glorious as those grade-school spring mornings when I was allowed to exchange long stockings for anklets. May was the time to sniff and touch flowers, roll in the grass, listen to Schubert on the radio, and profess undying love.

Of course, May had its dark side too. Grandma said that kittens born in May nearly always died before they became cats. She spoke of something that didn't work out as a "May cat." Suddenly I felt sorry for myself because I had to get up early and go to work while most of my friends slept deep into a Saturday morning. Those same friends would spend the summer collecting a college wardrobe while I typed letters and legal documents. In September, they would go off to unimaginable delights while I labored on.

In contrast with the brightness of the morning, the windowless law office seemed gloomier than usual. Volumes of the *Iowa Code Annotated* on the shelves looked like maroon tombstones. I looked years into the future and saw a woman in a drab skirt and what Grandma called a waist seated at the typewriter. Her tightly laced brown oxfords were planted in precise parallels, her hair was pulled back in a knot, and her fingers were ringless. She was me.

"Good morning, Margaret."

I saw the shoes first. Mr. Sommer always wore black shoes made in England, and the two-toned brown and white footgear startled me.

He flexed one foot and laughed. "My salute to the season, and speaking of that, I'll have to be looking for another girl. Can you recommend someone?"

My heart lurched as I realized what he was saying. I had taken my job for granted, going so far as to despise it, and now it was being snatched away? The somber office suddenly became dear to me. I loved the smell of the bookbindings and the carbon paper. I appreciated the rich wine shade of the law books. I wanted to wrap my arms around the old L.C. Smith typewriter and never let go. I was afraid.

Mr. Sommer watched me closely with the bright, quizzical look that usually signalled that a lesson was about to be taught, but I was too disturbed to interpret his expression. Tears welled in my eyes.

"Margaret, Margaret," he said, "when will you ever learn not to react until all the facts are in?"

"Wh—what facts?"

He sighed. "You're forcing me to reveal a carefully kept secret. Oh, well, it's probably better than having you break down and blubber during a public event."

"I always thought I'd go on working for you—I—" My voice quavered embarrassingly, and I fell silent.

He looked at me, and I remembered the feeling of leaving the Beekman farm in disgrace and of hearing the detasseling foreman say, "Don't come back." Now this: "I'll have to be looking for another girl." How could I ever tell Mom and Grandma? If I left the house every morning and spent the day somewhere, they wouldn't have to know for awhile, but where could I go in a town this size? How could I explain the absence of a paycheck indefinitely?

"Margaret," he finally said, "I don't see how you can work for me and go to college at the same time."

"But I'm not—I can't. I mean, I can't go to college."

"Not even with the Garner scholarship?"

Each year, as a memorial to a son who died in the war, the Garner family awarded to a graduating senior enough money for books and tuition at the State University of Iowa. I *couldn't* be getting it, because it always went to somebody in college prep. I shook my head in disbelief.

"I'm on the selection committee," he said.

This was another unbelievable piece of information. The Garners never revealed the number or identities of their selectors, but Sommer seemed an unlikely choice. He was nodding and telling me that his reputation for truth and veracity in the community was excellent.

"But I took the commercial course. They never—"

"I flatter myself that your association with me has been a liberal education."

I began to believe him—enough to make a timid inquiry about costs above and beyond the scholarship items.

He waved his hand airily. "That's where your typing and shorthand come in. You can get a part-time job. Margaret, do you want to go to college so much that you'd sleep in a culvert and raid garbage cans if you had to?"

I nodded with a trace of doubt, hearing Davy say, "Beg, borrow, or steal!"

"Then it's all settled. I'll talk to your mother if you think that will help. Just promise me one thing—"

"Anything!" Joy was bubbling up from my toes.

"When they make the announcement at commencement—Joe Garner will do it—for the love of God, act surprised. Carry on the way young girls are supposed to when you give them the moon. You might as well go home now, because I won't get any work out of you today, but I'll expect you Monday afternoon—and for the rest of the summer. And remember, this is a secret. Don't tell even your mother."

Taking the dim stairs three steps at a time, I was outside before I realized that I couldn't go home. Showing up when I should be working would raise all kinds of questions I couldn't answer without lying.

I started to run, feeling weightless in the cotton dress. It occurred to me that a prayer of thanks was in order. It should be offered in a church, but the blond woodwork and Palmolive odor of sanctity of my own church didn't seem right for the occasion. The quaint, old Episcopal church with the crimson doors was better. Two more blocks.

Nobody ever locked a church door in Harlan. I walked into soft, tawny light from mullioned windows and sank into a back pew to recover from the sideache I always got when I ran. The church had the same mysterious richness that had struck me in the Edelstein house. This was what I craved—decoration, complication, highlights, and shadows—more than could be seen with one swift glance. Without the familiar Jesus picture to focus my prayer, I simply said, "Thank You!" over and over.

Then I tried to imagine what the State University of Iowa might be like. I'd never been there and hadn't even looked at the catalogs, not wanting to see what I couldn't have. For the first time, I dared to think of myself as a college girl: carrying books, going to dances, sitting in a stadium. The backdrop was hazy, but Margaret Langelund, college girl, was well defined. This time, I would be the real thing, caught up in my college existence rather than standing aside to watch myself go through the motions.

My reverie was interrupted by the janitor (the Episcopalians call him a sexton), who was Mary Lois Engle's uncle. He knew me and looked so surprised that I felt guilty about being where I didn't belong. I hurried out and headed back toward the Square.

A new dress shop had opened in the space where Fern's Fashion had been. Usually I turned away when I passed it, fighting the memory of the day when Fern and Chet were carried through the front door. This time happiness was my shield, and I looked.

The Frockery was owned by Mardee Kreutzer, the wife of the new sale barn auctioneer. Rumor had it that Mardee had been a dancer in a Council Bluffs nightclub, but Mom thought people just jumped to that conclusion because she peroxided her hair and smoked cigarettes.

It could have been the May morning, my marvelously reopened future, the mere fact of being seventeen, or any combination of those factors, but I had to have the dress in the window. It was royal purple with a draped and swagged skirt further beautified with silver sequin butterflies.

I entered the shop in a trance, scarcely aware of the changes that had been made since Fern's day. Mardee herself asked if she could help me, and I simply pointed toward the window.

"The purple? You want to try it on?"

I nodded, not thinking to ask the size or the price, and Mardee climbed into the window where I had dressed mannequins in Fern's awful styles. One hand with long, red nails held the marvelous garment out to me while she used the other to cover the dummy's temporary nudity. I knew she didn't believe I'd come to buy. I was into the dress before she joined me in the fitting room and before I realized that remodeling had positioned the stall where Fern's bed had stood. When the thought struck me, I was glad for the sound of Mardee's voice.

"That looks good on you, honey, whyn't you come out and see yourself in the big mirror?"

I did, and the dress was beautiful. Never mind that I was wearing saddle shoes with it, never mind what it might cost, never mind anything at all. When I looked into the mirror, I saw Hedy Lamarr.

"Wouldn't have to do a thing to it," Mardee said. "Got a big occasion coming up?"

I nodded. The big occasion was my whole life. Then it occurred to me that I hadn't uttered a word since I entered the shop. Mardee would think I was (in the words of Mrs. Hess) "deef and dumb." I asked the price, and her answer shocked me into further silence.

"I could put it on lay-away."

"No, I want it today. Will you let me charge it? If you don't trust me, you can call Mr. Sommer."

"The lawyer on the east side of the Square?"

I nodded, terrified by my own audacity. I'd never charged anything in my life. Mom never bought anything until she could pay for it.

Mardee was willing to trust me. She folded the purple dress tenderly in tissue paper and put it into a big box distinguished by the name of the shop and the silhouette of a stylish lady. I didn't see how I could hide such a box and asked for a bag instead. Then I signed my name on the slip that said *Chg.*, feeling that I had made a pact with the devil.

The purple dress was my secret until just before the commencement ceremonies. It came to light when Mom spilled Lady Esther powder on her white gloves and went into the Farley bedroom to look for another pair.

The night was full of secrets. I was worrying about getting out of the house with the carnation corsage I'd bought at Gregory's Greenhouse to wear on my graduation robe. Mom had made it very clear that she disapproved of flowers on such garb, but everyone else was doing it, and I didn't want her to be embarrassed when I came down the aisle looking uncherished. She wasn't to know until the processional, and then it would be a *fait accompli.* I was practicing holding the flower box beneath the carefully pressed robe draped on my arm when the trumpet of doom sounded from the Farley bedroom.

"Margaret, what *is* this?" She flung the double doors wide and held the dress between two fingers as if it were a distasteful object. Grandma, who was fastening her mother-of-pearl circle pin to her dress, turned to look and quickly covered her eyes with one hand.

What could I say? The dress was the token of something I could not tell her about—a celebration. In another hour I could explain, but not now.

"Can we talk about it later? We should start for the school right now."

She gave me a long, hard look and draped the purple glory over the back of a dining room chair.

Grandma said, "Remember when I found that dress of Else's? When she was trying to be somebody she wasn't?"

"Now that you mention it, I do," Mom said.

The three of us walked to the school in silence. Aunt Kam and Uncle Karl were waiting in the vestibule, and the four of them went to find seats in the auditorium while I headed for the girls' restroom to put on my cap and gown and affix the smuggled carnations.

Mary Lois Engle was moving her lips silently as she gave her valedictorian's speech to the mirror. Wyonne was trying to decide which end of her orchid was up and which was down. Monica was grousing about how hard it was to keep stocking seams straight when you had skinny legs. Merrilee breezed in with a shoulderful of pink roses and told me they were from Donny. "That kid has been scrounging pop bottles and taking them to the store for months to get the money," she said. "Can you beat it?"

We lined up in the hall, and with the opening bars of Elgar's "Pomp and Circumstance," Merrilee Adams and the long, double column of Andersens entered the auditorium. That marvelous, majestic music made me believe I could do anything—even walk past my mother wearing forbidden flowers.

Mom was on the aisle, and she turned expectantly as the first Ls passed. Her eyes met mine proudly, bounced to the flowers, and returned to my face with an ominous glitter. When Grandma saw the flowers, her lips curved in a tiny smile for an instant. Because she didn't understand the situation, Aunt Kam smiled guilelessly and poked Uncle Karl to be sure he didn't miss me.

I scarcely heard what Mary Lois had to say or what the bank president talked about, but when Joe Garner got up to speak, I came to rigid attention. He said his son Kevin was a brilliant boy whose flame was snuffed out too soon and that he and Mrs. Garner were determined to light a new flame to his memory each year by helping a young person with aspirations.

"This year," he said, "our selection committee has chosen a young woman from a pioneer family. When we speak of the pioneers, the image of a man breaking the prairie comes to mind, but in this case, we must think of strong women who struggled against harsh circumstances to raise worthy children."

Feeling most unworthy, I squirmed in my seat. Mr. Sommer was watching me, waiting to see how I would handle the big moment. When Joe Garner said my name, I threw my head back, dropping my mortar board into the lap of the Miller boy. He gave it back to me, and I smiled and even cried a little while everybody clapped. I hoped that I was carrying on the way young girls are supposed to when you give them the moon.

Somehow I managed to get through the rest of the ceremony, but I scarcely remembered walking across the stage to take my diploma from the hand of the high school principal. Mrs. Cooper repeated the Elgar piece for the recessional, and we rushed to return the caps and gowns to the rental people.

Merrilee said, "Well, it's all over for me, but not for you, I guess."

"I can't believe it."

Neither could my family, but Aunt Kam and Uncle Karl came to our house for lemonade and excited talk about what had to be done to get me into the University of Iowa. I listened quietly, preoccupied with the coming hour of reckoning. I wondered which Mom would tackle first, the corsage or the purple dress?

Was no joy ever pure? Here I was wearing my very first wristwatch (Mom's gift), a necklace with a single golden rose from Aunt Kam and Uncle Karl, and flowers on my shoulder. I was as festively adorned as I'd ever been, but I was miserable. The girl graduate in a white dress reflected in the dining room window was a whited sepulchre. Inside of her was a black-haired wench in a clinging purple dress.

When Aunt Kam and Uncle Karl left, I offered to wash the dishes, but Mom said, "Wait until morning. It's late."

I started to unpin the corsage, bracing myself for the worst, but she opened a drawer and handed me a cellophane bag that had been washed and reused repeatedly. "Put them in this, and they'll keep quite awhile in the Norge."

I felt uneasy, cheated of expiation, and I said, "I can take the dress back."

"No, keep it. In time, that dress will tell you something." She kissed my forehead. "Good night, Margaret, I'm very proud of you."

Tears smarted in my eyes as I put the flowers in the refrigerator between a jar of pickles and a covered bowl of fruit soup, my favorite Danish dish.

I was ready to turn out the light and climb into bed when I heard a tap at the door.

"Margrethe?"

Grandma stepped into my room in her long, muslin nightgown. The coiled braid of her hair had been released to hang down her back like a Chinaman's pigtail. She said, "You probably thought I had no gift for you."

"I hadn't thought," I said honestly, because she wasn't in the habit of giving things.

"I want you to have this." She opened her hand, revealing a circle of gold.

"But that's your wedding ring—"

"Peter would approve." She pushed it on my ring finger, and it was too big, so she put it on the middle finger. "Such little hands! What will you do with those little hands?"

"I don't know, Grandma, but *something!*"

She nodded. "Sail out, Margaret, it's time."

I smiled. "But not farther than I can row back?"

She drew herself up with all the dignity of her eighty-seven years and slashed the air with a gnarled hand. "Don't worry about the rowing back, just *sail!*" With that, she left me.

I stared at the circlet of mellow, Danish gold for a moment before I pulled the purple dress from the closet. The ring on my hand made the dress look cheap. I climbed into bed and thought, and the thought became a hope, and the hope became a boat that carried me to the land of my heart's desire. Sailing out—sailing out at last.